GONE TO GROUND

A DETECTIVE KAY HUNTER CRIME THRILLER

RACHEL AMPHLETT

SAXON
PUBLISHING

ONE

Lee Temple let the carbon-framed bicycle coast to a slower speed, turning his ankles outwards to release his shoe cleats from the pedals as the tyres met the rough surface.

He braked next to one of the other riders, noting the look of annoyance that flitted across Nigel Simpson's face.

'Puncture?'

'Second one this week,' said Nigel. 'At this rate, this tyre is going to be shredded.'

'Have you got a spare tube?'

'Yes, thanks. It's a pain, that's all.'

Lee emitted a noncommittal grunt, then glanced over his shoulder as the rest of the group pulled into the lay-by.

The group of four men had started their cycling club eight months ago, and he had been surprised at how fast his fitness levels had improved. Considering that the idea had been first broached over a pint in their local pub one night, they had taken to the new pastime with enthusiasm, much to the amusement of their wives who had given them three months at most before they grew bored.

Over time, they had learned where the best cafés were, and Lee salivated at the thought of the sausage roll he intended to devour at their favourite spot on the other side of Boughton Monchelsea. Not that he would tell his wife – she thought the bowl of cereal he had consumed an hour before would be enough to satiate his appetite and keep his diet on track.

The ride had started well – the route was a favourite one, and perfect for a summer Sunday morning. They had avoided the busy traffic through Maidstone, meeting up at six-thirty when the air was still cool, having set off from West Farleigh. Their route had seen them leave the busy town centre and follow the road south towards Langley before turning west along a quiet country lane.

'How's that new carbon frame holding up?'

He flinched at the heavy hand on his shoulder and forced a smile.

Paul Banks was a heavyset man and unaware of his own strength. Lee often thought that the man should be playing rugby, rather than trying to perch on a lightweight bicycle frame, but he never seemed to have any trouble keeping up with the group.

'Yeah, good. I can really notice the difference,' Lee said, failing to keep the sense of pride out of his voice.

'Maybe now Heather will see it was worth the money.'

'She will, once I've sold the golf clubs to pay for it.'

Paul laughed, slapped him on the shoulder once more, and wheeled his bike across to where the other men were conversing.

The golf clubs were the residual evidence of the last attempt the group had had at getting fit.

Lee's interest in cycling had been piqued years before, when the initial stage of the Tour de France had passed through the county. When he had suggested it to the others, they'd made disparaging remarks about tight Lycra and laughed it off, but once he'd presented them with enough evidence to suggest it would keep them fit and give them a good excuse to get out of the house for a few hours on a Sunday morning, they had soon joined him.

Now, they all looked forward to the weekly event and today was no different.

He removed his sunglasses and wiped at them with a corner of his cycling jersey, squinting against the bright sunlight that crested the hedgerow beyond. Rarely used by heavy vehicles, the lane was awash with the sound of birdsong.

He glanced back at Nigel, who now had the front wheel of his bike on the ground while he wedged tyre levers over the rim. Paul had crouched down to help him, and it looked like they were going to be there for at least another ten minutes or so.

A sudden urge to piss created an ache in his abdomen and, tucking his sunglasses over the collar of his jersey, he walked away from the group.

'Where are you off to?' said Tony White as he passed him.

The hospital orderly wore the latest aerodynamic helmet, and Lee noticed his reflection in the rainbow-coloured lenses of the other man's sunglasses.

'Need to take a leak.'

The other man grinned. 'Pit stop. Might as well make the most of it.'

'Exactly.'

Lee wandered over to the far side of the lay-by,

then noticed the discarded work boot on the verge next to the road.

He had always wondered why you only ever saw one single boot at the side of the road, and not two. His childhood imagination had envisaged a man walking around with only one boot, at a loss as to what had happened to the other.

Paul's voice reached him at the same time he drew level with the footwear.

'Piss in it!'

Lee chuckled under his breath and shook his head.

'Go on. Dare you,' called Tony.

A bluebottle fly landed on his cheek, and he waved it away as a barrage of laughter carried across from the other men.

Then he blinked and shook his head, bile rising in his throat.

He stared for a moment, the others' jeers fading into a blur of white noise. A car swept past, its motion rocking his body as he stood, arms by his side, trying to comprehend why it was here, who it belonged to, and what he should do.

At last, his brain processed what his eyes were taking in.

A severed foot, cut off at the ankle.

A pool of congealed blood pulsated with flies that

buzzed around the torn laces of the leather upper of the work boot.

He took a step back, his anguished cry silencing the others.

His heart racing, he twisted his ankle as he turned away, his shoe cleats slipping across the uneven surface, before he limped to the hedgerow and threw up his meagre breakfast.

TWO

Detective Inspector Kay Hunter eased open the passenger door of the pool vehicle and surveyed the scene before her.

She'd received a call from Detective Chief Inspector Devon Sharp as she and her partner, Adam, had been having a lazy weekend brunch on the patio overlooking their garden on the outskirts of Maidstone.

'This is exactly the sort of sensationalist story we don't need on the front page of the newspapers,' he said. 'I want you to lead this one – Barnes can be your deputy SIO, given that we still haven't got a new detective sergeant assigned to the team. I'll have him pick you up as soon as possible.'

Kay had sensed the familiar spike of an adrenalin rush caused by the prospect of a new investigation.

She had to give the newly promoted DCI credit, too. Since her promotion to DI, Sharp had ensured that she got the opportunity to work on a number of high profile investigations in between her management obligations.

Detective Constable Ian Barnes had turned up on her doorstep twenty-five minutes after Sharp ended his phone call.

Kay enjoyed working with Barnes. In his late forties, he possessed a humour and fortitude that had been a welcome tonic to the dark crimes they were often faced with.

Now, standing beside their vehicle as she peered up the lane to where a strip of crime scene tape fluttered in the breeze, she turned to him as he slammed the driver's door shut and joined her.

A little taller than Kay, he had pale brown hair that had turned to grey at his temples, and much to his consternation, he had started to wear reading glasses.

'Still glad to be out of the office?' he said as they watched the scene-of-crime officers working in the lay-by.

'Shame about the circumstances,' she said, and pushed a strand of her blonde hair behind her ear. She straightened her shoulders. 'All right. Let's go and find out what's going on.'

She made her way up the sloping gradient of the lane, nodding to the traffic officers who kept passing motorists from gawking at the scene and ensured any passing traffic remained at a constant low speed to avoid injury to the emergency responders attending the site.

The crime scene investigation team had erected a screen between the lane and where they worked, while two uniformed officers stood on the perimeter of the crime scene tape to ward off any nosy passers-by. A female uniformed officer and her colleague had corralled a group of garishly-clothed cyclists and glanced up as Kay and Barnes approached.

Kay relaxed as she recognised the familiar face. Debbie West had been a police constable since her early twenties, and Kay held high hopes for the woman. She was one of the most meticulous officers Kay knew and could be relied upon to manage a tight crime scene.

'Morning, Inspector.'

'Morning. What's the latest?'

Debbie gestured to her colleague, who shepherded the cyclists away from the crime scene tape and continued to speak with them as he took notes. She turned back to Kay.

'The guy in the red and yellow jersey is the one that found it. Lee Temple. Apparently, he and his friends are all local to West Farleigh and cycle together on a regular basis at weekends.'

Kay squinted against the bright sunshine to where the man stood next to Debbie's colleague, and noted the line of expensive bicycles propped up against a telegraph pole or laid on the thick grass that bordered the road.

'How is he doing?'

'Threw up his breakfast, but thankfully not on the evidence.'

'That's something, I suppose.'

Barnes jerked his chin towards where the CSIs were painstakingly checking the verges and hedgerow bordering the lay-by, their heads bowed as they worked.

'Have they found the rest of him?'

Debbie wrinkled her nose. 'Not yet.'

Kay checked over her shoulder at the steady stream of traffic that now passed the crime scene, and had to agree with Sharp's view that the media would be keen to have the story on the six o'clock news that night, with whatever scant information they'd glean from witnesses.

'I take it you've warned Mr Temple and his associates not to speak to anyone about this?'

'Absolutely,' said Debbie.

Barnes tapped Kay on the arm at a shout from beyond the taped-off area, and she turned to see one of the CSI officers beckoning to them.

'I'd like to speak to Mr Temple before you let him go,' she said to Debbie.

'No problem. I was going to organise a taxi mini-van to take them all home. Can't imagine they'd want to ride back after this.'

'Good thinking, thanks. Back in a minute.' She followed Barnes to the perimeter tape and hovered at the temporary boundary. 'Morning, Harriet.'

'Morning. Debbie said you two were on your way over.'

Kay noted the weariness in the crime scene investigator's voice and resolved to let her get on with the task at hand as soon as possible.

'What can you tell us?'

Harriet handed them a set of disposable overalls and waited while they donned them and placed the matching bootees over their shoes, then held aloft the tape for them to duck under before leading them behind the screen towards the far end of the lay-by via a demarcated path.

'Before you ask, the only footprints we've lifted from here match the cyclists' shoes – pretty easy to deduce because of the cleats they were wearing to clip into their pedals.'

The CSI officer slowed as she reached the work boot.

It seemed incongruous in its position next to the long grass of the verge now that they knew what it contained, and yet Kay recounted numerous occasions where she'd seen similar lone shoes discarded at the side of a road and had thought nothing of it.

She crouched a metre or so away from the boot and batted a fly away from her face as Harriet continued.

'Our victim is definitely male based on what we can see without removing the footwear. The boot is made from quality leather, but worn, as if it were one of a favourite pair. The heel has been eroded on one side, but Lucas will be able to tell you more about characteristics of our victim once he's taken a look at it.'

Kay mumbled a response. She'd worked with Lucas Anderson, the Home Office pathologist on previous occasions, and his attention to detail and tenacity in providing as much information as possible about a victim had helped her more than once.

She didn't doubt his ability to add more to the picture of the victim that they needed to create if they were to find the person responsible.

'And no sign of any other parts?'

'No – we've almost concluded our preliminary search. Obviously, I'll let you know if anything changes.'

'How long has it been out here, do you think?'

'Hard to say, to be honest. A lot of the dirt and dust on the leather uppers has been caused by passing traffic as much as the bad weather we've had at the beginning of the month. Again, Lucas might be able to pinpoint a rough time of death for you to help to narrow it down.'

Kay straightened and turned to Barnes, whose upper lip curled as he watched the flies congregating upon the bloody stump. She spun on her heel and craned her neck until she could see beyond the screen and to the lane that disappeared in a straight line in each direction.

'We'll need to speak to homeowners along this stretch of road. You never know – they might have security cameras.'

Barnes nodded. 'I'll speak to Debbie to get

uniform to start that straight away. I'll give Gavin and Carys a call this afternoon to make sure they're in early tomorrow morning, too.'

They moved back to the perimeter of the crime scene, and as she stripped the protective coveralls from her clothes and handed them to one of Harriet's assistants, Kay let her gaze rest on the amputated foot once more.

'Who the hell are you?' she muttered.

THREE

Debbie and her colleague paused in their interviewing as Kay and Barnes approached, then introduced them to the four cyclists.

Kay noted the washed-out pallor of Lee Temple's features, and the almost sheepish expressions his friends wore.

It never ceased to amaze her that witnesses to a crime would often feel guilty about what they had seen, despite having no other involvement.

Or maybe it was simply the effect of being surrounded by uniformed police officers and crime scene investigators.

She turned her focus to Temple and eased him away from the others.

'Mr Temple, I'm DI Kay Hunter and this is my

colleague, DC Ian Barnes. I understand it was you who first found the work boot?'

He nodded, then swallowed and Kay automatically stepped back in case the man was about to vomit once more.

He flapped his hand as if to ward off the sensation. 'I'm all right, it's okay.'

'You've had a terrible shock, and you're doing really well,' she said. 'I realise you and your friends have spoken to PC West, but I'd like to have a word before we get you all home.'

She glanced to the right of him as a liveried minivan drew to a standstill a little way off from the lay-by and the driver applied the hazard lights, before turning her attention back to Temple.

'Tell you what, let's get your friends and all your bikes into the taxi, and then me and Barnes will drive you home once we've had a chat.'

He let out a shaking breath, then ran his hand over mid-length dark brown hair that had been flattened by the helmet he now cradled in his hands. 'Okay, thanks.'

The three other cyclists were full of concern for their friend as they shook his hand and then followed the uniformed officers towards the taxi.

'I'll pop round later to see you,' said the taller of

the men, before he picked up a second bicycle from the grass verge and wheeled it over to the taxi.

Kay watched while Temple raised his hand in farewell as the vehicle pulled back out into the lane, his expression wistful.

'Guv? We've got company.'

Kay spun on her heel at Barnes's words, and stifled a groan at the sight of a familiar figure extricating himself from a four-door car that had been parked further up the lane from the lay-by.

Despite the distance between them, she could sense the excitement emanating from Jonathan Aspley as he hurried towards the crime tape on the far side of the screen.

'Get Lee to the car, Ian. Be with you in a moment.'

She intercepted the reporter as he drew level with the screen and turned him away from the direction of Barnes's car.

'Now is not a good time, Aspley.'

'Come on, Hunter – before the rest of them get here. At least give me a quote I can use.'

Kay narrowed her eyes. 'Trust me, you won't be able to print what I say if you don't back off. There will be a media conference later today at headquarters. Come along to that, and I'll give you as much information as I can then.'

'And I'll simply end up with the same story as everybody else. You owe me.'

'I do not.' She sighed. 'Look, it's too early for this. Be at the press conference later on, let my team get on with their jobs now, and I'll see what I can send your way in a couple of days.'

'Exclusive?'

'That'll be up to Sharp, but I'll do my best.'

'You mean, you'll use me if you need to drip feed information.'

'I can give it to one of your competitors, if you like?'

His mouth thinned. 'I'll see you later.'

Kay waited until he had reached his car, then spun on her heel and hurried back to where Barnes sat in his vehicle, Lee Temple on the back seat.

'Sorry about that.' Kay reached into her bag for her notebook and a pen before twisting around in her seat. 'Okay, I know that you've already spoken to our uniformed colleagues about what you found, Lee, but please could you take me through what happened this morning? Tell me everything, even if you think it isn't important.'

He bit his lip, then nodded and proceeded to

describe his time from leaving his house that morning up until he'd discovered the grisly remains in the work boot. His friend, Tony White, had been the one to phone triple nine.

Kay remained silent as he talked, taking notes and jotting down his responses to her questions while she listened.

Although Debbie and her colleague had taken initial witness statements from the four cyclists, Kay preferred to hear accounts from witnesses herself whenever possible. Often, someone like Lee would remember a detail the second time around that hadn't been mentioned before as his mind continued to process what he had been through.

When he had finished speaking, she gave him a moment to collect himself, then cleared her throat.

'When you were approaching the lay-by, did you notice any vehicles?'

'No – we had the road to ourselves. We were riding side by side, with me and Nigel in front. Nigel got the lead on me, before he noticed he had a puncture. That's when we pulled off the road. There were no vehicles in front of us, and the first time I noticed one was after I'd found the boot.'

'Is this a favourite route of yours?' said Barnes.

'It was,' Lee mumbled, then dropped his gaze and turned his cycling helmet over in his hands.

'How long have you been coming this way?' said Kay.

'About eight months.'

'Ever seen someone in that lay-by?'

'I'm sorry – I can't remember.'

'That's okay. What sort of vehicles do you see along here?'

'Normal ones, I suppose. Cars, motorbikes. Sometimes a van, perhaps. It's usually quiet along this stretch. It's why we come this way.' His forehead puckered. 'I'm not being very helpful, am I?'

'You're doing fine,' said Kay. 'It all helps us.'

'Okay.'

'When did you last cycle along here?'

'About four weeks ago.'

'Did you notice anything then? Anything that seemed out of place?'

'No – we only stopped today because Nigel got that puncture. Otherwise—'

She saw Barnes raise his eyebrow as she dropped her notebook back into her bag and nodded.

There would be no more questions for Lee Temple today. She would let the man rest, then speak to him again in a day or so, to see if time had added anything to his memories of the route and the circumstances in which he'd discovered the work boot.

Kay fastened her seatbelt. 'What's your address, Lee?'

The cyclist rattled it off, and Barnes nodded in recognition, before accelerating away from the crime scene.

Half an hour later, Barnes flicked the indicator as he slowed the vehicle, then turned left into a lane that led around the back of West Farleigh and past the train station.

He braked to a gentle halt at a row of terraced houses, then climbed from the car and opened the back door for Temple. He handed him a business card before sending the man on his way and sliding behind the steering wheel once more.

'Poor bastard,' he muttered.

Kay bit her lip as she watched the door to the house open wide.

A woman appeared, her dark blonde hair swept up into a ponytail and a little girl balanced on her hip.

Lee staggered over the threshold and into the woman's embrace. They remained there for a moment, and then she led him inside and shut the door.

Barnes released the handbrake and edged the car away from the kerb.

'I don't think Mr Temple will be doing much cycling for the foreseeable future.'

'I can't say I blame him,' said Kay. 'I'd imagine he's going to be having nightmares for a while yet.'

FOUR

Kay unbuttoned her shirtsleeves and rolled them up until they reached her elbows.

The morning had turned warm by the time they'd reached Maidstone police station, while the cloudless skies above provided a perfect summer's day.

Though they would all prefer to be at home with their families, she knew the team would now be focusing on the tasks at hand. She was pleased that she and Barnes had been on call, otherwise the crime scene would have been handed over to someone else, and she would have been stuck in a three-day workshop entitled "Advanced Management Techniques" from Monday morning.

Her relief was tempered by the thought that someone could have been injured or died in horrific circumstances, and she would do all she could to bring the person responsible to justice.

The incident room buzzed with activity when she pushed through the door and crossed to her desk. Phillip Parker had taken the initiative to set up a whiteboard and source extra computers while she and Barnes had been at the crime scene.

She'd first met the constable when he was completing his probationary period twelve months ago, and it was evident that, under the tutelage of PC Norris, the young man was settling into his role well. He'd filled out, too – where once he'd been a lanky twenty-something, he'd added weight to his slight frame and Kay realised he'd probably done so to take on some of Maidstone's more colourful characters.

Friday and Saturday nights could be a menace in the town centre, and Parker would have surely been a target for troublemakers.

'Great work, Phil,' she said as she approached.

He grinned. 'Thought it'd save some time.'

'Thanks.'

She peered over her shoulder at the rest of the assembled team.

At present, there were only four other uniformed officers assisting, but that would change in the morning once rosters were adjusted and help gleaned from other investigations.

She wouldn't be popular, that was for sure.

Kay resolved to take her fellow detectives out for a drink in a few weeks to soften the blow of losing resources to her murder case, and then turned her attention to the whiteboard.

Parker had printed out a large colour map of the Maidstone area, the location of the morning's bloody discovery already highlighted with a large red pin. He'd obtained images of the lane via online mapping software and had pinned these next to the map.

They would suffice until the scene-of-crime officers provided their own photographs.

Once satisfied that the administrative side of the investigation was organised, she returned to her desk and flicked through her notebook until she found Lee Temple's interview and began to type up her scrawl.

A new investigation would be set up in the HOLMES database by a specially assigned officer later on that day, and she would add her interview to the growing amount of collated information, beginning the process of enquiry.

She glanced up as Barnes sank into the chair opposite her desk and wiggled his mouse to wake up his computer.

'Have you spoken to Gavin and Carys?'

'Yes – they'll be in at seven tomorrow. They both offered to come in today, if you want them to?'

'No, that's okay. I'd rather they rest today – goodness knows when they'll next get time off, and we need everybody to be focused on this one.'

She looked up as DCI Sharp approached their desks, the senior detective exuding an air of efficiency that he had carried with him from his time in the military, then years spent as a detective in the Kent Police area.

'What can you tell me?' he said.

'First off, we're going to need to organise a press conference for this afternoon,' said Kay. 'Jonathan Aspley from the *Kentish Times* turned up as we were leaving with the witness, and he won't be the only one sniffing around for a story. We need to manage this from the start to avoid the media creating panic and speculation.'

Sharp ran a hand over his close-cropped silver flecked hair and sighed. 'I agree – I would rather have left it a day or so, but with the crime scene in such a public place, I'm surprised we haven't seen anything on social media yet.'

'The first responders and Harriet's team did a great job of shielding the area from passing cars, guv,'

27

GONE TO GROUND   27

said Barnes. 'No-one will be able to get anything on camera, anyway.'

'They're keeping a look-out for drones, and I know for a fact that the local news helicopter is in for servicing this week,' said Kay, 'so no-one is going to get an aerial shot, either.'

'Good.' Sharp turned and pulled a chair over, lowering himself into it before speaking again. 'I understand there were four cyclists, and one of them found the boot?'

'Yes, Lee Temple,' said Kay. 'Works as a primary school teacher in Paddock Wood. Lives in West Farleigh, and he and his three mates cycle together every Sunday morning. The lane is a regular route of theirs to get to Boughton Monchelsea, but this was the first time in four months they had ever stopped in that lay-by.'

'So, any idea how long that severed foot has been there for?'

'Harriet was reluctant to hazard a guess. Hopefully, Lucas Anderson will be able to tell us more when he does the post mortem.'

Sharp nodded and leaned back in his chair. 'You can both appreciate that we are going to be under the microscope with this one. Especially as the team is still missing a detective sergeant role since your promotion, Kay. We've got interviews lined up for next week, and you're going to be expected to sit in on some of those, so make sure you factor that into the tasks you set everyone.' He raised an eyebrow at Barnes. 'Are you sure we can't persuade you to apply?'

Barnes's mouth twisted at the corner. 'No thanks, guv.'

Sharp shrugged. 'It was worth a shot.'

He didn't say anything further, but Kay could sense his disappointment in Barnes's decision. Often, it was easier to recruit from within an established team than bring a new person on board and hope that it didn't upset the dynamics between existing personnel.

On the other hand, she respected Barnes's decision – there was no sense in him taking on the role if he wasn't happy to do so. They were sharing the detective sergeant duties between them in the interim, but they wouldn't be able to sustain it – not with a murder enquiry underway.

She couldn't blame Sharp for trying – she'd mentioned the role to Barnes last week when they'd sneaked out of the incident room and taken their lunch down to a favourite spot next to the river behind the Bishop's Palace.

He'd been adamant, though, and said he was content to stay as a detective constable.

Sharp rose from his chair and tucked it out of the way under another desk. 'Right, I'll let you both get on. Kay – expect to be at headquarters for four o'clock this afternoon so we can do this press conference together. I'll see you in the morning, Barnes.'

'Guv.'

Kay turned away at a *ping* from her computer and wheeled closer to the screen. 'Harriet's just emailed through the initial photographs from the scene, Ian.'

Barnes moved around the desks to join her, and they flicked through the images.

As she cast her gaze over the shocking scene depicted in the photos, she couldn't help wondering what he had done to deserve such a brutal end.

'What sort of person does that?' said Barnes.

She closed the last attachment and rubbed at her right eye. 'More to the point, where was he taking it, and where's the rest?'

FIVE

Kay's first impression was one of pure pandemonium as she strode into the large meeting room that had been seconded for the afternoon press conference.

It appeared that word had travelled fast amongst the Kentish news corp, with all the chairs taken up and news cameramen and photographers jostling for space along the walls.

She wrinkled her nose at the faint aroma of stale cigarettes that clung to the reporters' clothing as she moved down the aisle towards the dais where a long table had been set up.

Joanne Thomas, an administrative assistant from headquarters who had been brought in to help with the press conference, had told Kay that some of the reporters had turned up an hour before to ensure they got a front row seat, and Kay wondered how many of them were now gasping for their next nicotine fix.

The noise level was deafening as she dumped her handbag behind the table and faced the room.

Six months ago, she'd been terrified at the thought of facing all those people, the camera lenses with their unblinking eyes upon her and the worry that she'd somehow slip up and make a mistake.

Now, she ran a practised eye over the gathered throng, taking her time and sizing up her audience.

She nodded to a few familiar faces and ignored the scowl that a raven-haired female reporter shot her way – she'd had a run-in with Suzie Chambers a while back but was surprised to see her perched on one of the seats at the front. Usually, the woman worked as the local television news show's roving reporter, and Kay wondered if Chambers had annoyed her bosses somehow to be relegated to covering the murder investigation from this angle. As it was, she sat with a thunderous expression and her arms folded across her chest.

A commotion near the door caught Kay's attention, and she looked across to see Jonathan Aspley hurrying down the aisle, his neck craned as he sought out a spare chair.

The reporter's pale eyes locked with hers for a

moment, and he pushed his hair out of his eyes, before his head jerked sideways at a loud whistle to his left, and Kay saw another reporter wave Aspley over, indicating a seat next to him.

Grumbling ensued as the reporters stood to let him pass before the hubbub increased to its previous raucous level.

Kay turned back to her bag and extracted the notes she'd typed up in the incident room. The first page contained a statement she would read out, and included key points she wanted the media to report that she hoped would advance the fledgling investigation. The second page covered questions she expected to have to answer in such a way as to protect Lee Temple and his friends and included operational matters she preferred Sharp to address.

Often, his military bark would cow the most persistent journalist.

On cue, the door at the back of the room opened and the DCI appeared, straightening his tie and casting his gaze over the assembled media as he joined Kay behind the table.

'We'll give them another couple of minutes to make sure everyone's here, and then we'll make a start,' he said.

'Sounds good. This is what I've drawn up.'

He took the pages, his eyes skimming her words, then handed them back with a curt nod. 'Good work.'

He dragged the chair next to hers from its place against the table and sat down with an ill-disguised sigh.

'You all right?' Kay said out the corner of her mouth.

'Politics. As usual. You and I are going to have to manage this so we don't encroach too much on other caseloads – the chief superintendent has already got my nuts in a vice over how many extra staff I've managed to coerce from the Division.'

'I thought perhaps we could organise drinks for them after all this is done? Sort of make up for leaving them short of staff.'

'They'll bankrupt us and end up with cirrhosis of their livers.'

She stifled a laugh. Smiling at a press conference about a murder was never a good idea.

Sharp obviously thought the same thing, because he rose from his seat and bellowed over the noise.

'Ladies and gentlemen – kindly take your seats and we'll begin.'

The effect was immediate, with the entire press corp silenced. A faint murmur persisted at the back of the room until an older journalist swore and told the offending photographer to keep quiet, and then all eyes turned to Kay and Sharp.

Kay cleared her throat and peered at her notes, resisting the urge to blink as a phone camera's flash exploded with light from the front row.

'Earlier today, Kent Police were called to a lay-by on a lane east of Boughton Monchelsea,' she said. 'A group of cyclists reported that they had found human remains, and upon further investigation by crime scene officers, this was confirmed to be the case.'

She paused, sensing an overwhelming urge to interrupt emanating from the journalists before her. She glared at them and noticed a raised hand at the back of the room dropping from sight, its owner chastened.

'At this time, no further details can be shared. We can confirm that, as of an hour ago, the lane has been fully reopened at the conclusion of our search of the area. We wish to thank local residents for their patience during this time. We are in the very early stages of our investigation and will provide more details to you as and when that is possible. In the meantime, we would ask anyone with information to call the Crimestoppers number. I would remind everyone that all calls are treated anonymously.'

She lowered the page, and glanced across at

Sharp, who nodded before adjusting the microphone on the table in front of him.

'Detective Inspector Hunter will be leading the Kent Police investigation with my full support,' he said. 'Until such time as more information is to hand, we would ask that you do not speculate upon this discovery. At present, we are treating this as an isolated incident. Kay?'

'Thanks. Any questions?'

The hand at the back of the room shot up once more before anyone else had the chance.

'Yes?'

A bespectacled twenty-something rose to his feet, a notebook and pen in his hand.

Kay saw his mouth move but couldn't hear him over the murmured conversations nearest to her.

'Excuse me.' She rapped her knuckles on the microphone until the culprits fell silent. 'Thank you. This is going to go a lot quicker if you keep quiet while someone else is talking. Unless you want to miss your slot for the six o'clock news?'

A line of reproached faces glared back at her.

'Thank you. You were saying?'

'The location of the remains is only a few miles from police headquarters. Why did it take until now to discover them?'

All eyes turned on Kay, and she groaned inwardly. She knew the police would be criticised on this point but had hoped to have more news for the media before the question was raised.

'The remains, unfortunately, are not complete and were not found in a place frequented by the public,' she said, and turned her attention to a familiar face.

Jonathan Aspley managed a smile of thanks before speaking.

'The cyclists who found the remains – are they under suspicion?'

Kay swallowed. She had to choose her words carefully.

If the assembled media thought Lee Temple and his friends were fair game, the men and their families would suffer the indignity of being hounded until the case was solved.

'They are assisting us with our enquiries,' she said, 'and we would request that their privacy be respected at this time.'

She turned her attention to Susie Chambers and shot her a warning glare.

The woman had a reputation for sensationalist stories, and Kay resolved to ask one of the uniformed officers on the team to speak with the cyclists and advise them of their rights in case the journalist and her colleagues failed to heed Kay's admonishment.

As the press conference progressed, a repetitiveness crept into the questions and Kay held up her hand.

'That's all for today. Our media team will be in touch when we have more to report.'

She pushed back her chair, shoved her notes into her bag and hurried to follow Sharp through the door at the back of the room.

She sighed as it closed behind her, letting her shoulders relax, and shut her eyes as she eased a crick out of the neck muscles.

'Good work in there, Hunter,' said Sharp.

She blinked. 'Thanks, guv.'

'I'm sure they'll embellish it all a bit, but that can't be helped. Happens all the time.' He checked his watch and raised an eyebrow. 'You'd best get going. Early start tomorrow. Give my regards to Adam, won't you?'

'Thanks, guv.'

SIX

Kay pushed through the door to the incident room at half past six the next morning, a cardboard tray with four take-out coffee cups balanced in one hand and her mobile phone in the other.

It rang as she hurried towards her desk, and in her haste to answer it before it went to voicemail, her handbag slipped down her arm and hot coffee spilled over her hand. She cursed under her breath, dropped her handbag to the floor and reached out to a box of tissues as she hit the answer button and put the phone to her ear.

'Hunter.'

She dabbed at her hand with a tissue before mopping up the puddle on her desk, then tossed the sodden mess into a wastepaper basket at her feet and sank into her chair.

'It's Jonathan Aspley. I wondered if you had time for a chat?'

Kay sighed. 'I've got no more news for you, Jonathan. You heard everything we know at yesterday's press conference.'

'Oh, come on. You've got to give me more than that. My editor is expecting me to provide an update on our website before nine o'clock this morning – we're trying to get a head start on everyone else.'

Kay closed her eyes and forced herself to count to ten before answering.

'You're pushing your luck. Your ratings aren't my problem – I've got an investigation team descending on this office in fifteen minutes for a briefing. When we have more detail, our media liaison officer will be in touch.'

She ended the call before he could respond and slid the phone across her desk.

Kay had worked closely with the reporter before, but it was the first time he had tried to take advantage of their tentative friendship. She bit her lip. In future, she vowed to be more careful – she couldn't afford to be distracted.

She peered over her shoulder to Sharp's office, but the DCI was absent.

Since her promotion, she'd been able to convince him to stay put – she was happy at her desk, in the thick of all the goings-on in the incident room, and a reluctance to shut herself away from the throng of investigations kept her hoping he'd resist the temptation to move upstairs or, worse, to headquarters.

Her thoughts were interrupted by the arrival of two of her colleagues, Detective Constables Gavin Piper and Carys Miles.

Given the smart trouser suit the female officer wore and the determined expression on her face, Kay found it hard to recall that she had last seen Carys singing at the top of her lungs in a karaoke bar in the town centre on Saturday night while celebrating her thirtieth birthday. Kay hadn't said anything to Sharp, but it was partly why she hadn't insisted the two detectives attend the incident room twenty-four hours earlier.

Gavin Piper, the younger of the two detectives, still looked the worse for wear and for someone who had told Kay at the beginning of the celebrations that he didn't drink much, she remembered him knocking back tequila shots by the time she and Adam had left the bar and wobbled their way to a taxi rank.

She indicated the take-out coffees on her desk. 'I figured you'd need this.'

'Guv, you're a legend,' said Gavin, tearing open two sugar sachets and dumping them into the hot liquid, his spiky blonde hair even messier than usual.

'I take it you're both well rested?'

Carys's face paled against her dark hair. 'I'm never drinking again. I didn't wake up until midday yesterday, and I felt sick until nine o'clock last night.'

Gavin winked. 'It's because you're old now. No more late nights for you, missy.'

Kay laughed as Carys threw a stress ball at him, then turned as Barnes appeared at the door.

He ambled across to where she sat, and took the coffee she held out to him with a nod of thanks, his mouth twitching at the sight of the other two detectives.

'Ah, to be young and stupid again,' he drawled.

'Leave it out,' said Carys, stifling a yawn. 'Have any of you got some paracetamol?'

Kay reached into her desk, her hand seeking out the packet she kept in the top drawer, then stopped and glowered at Barnes as he sat opposite her. 'Have you been nicking stuff out of my desk again?'

He held up his hands. 'Don't look at me. I learned

my lesson after those bloody typing lessons you made me do when I borrowed your stapler.'

'Borrowed? I never saw it again!'

'I've got some,' said Gavin, and unzipped a pocket on the side of his backpack before tossing a packet to Carys.

Kay pushed back her chair as the room filled with uniformed officers and administrative staff, and gestured to the whiteboard at the end of the room. 'Come on, you lot. Let's get this show on the road.'

She led the way to the group of officers milling about near the whiteboard, nodded to some familiar faces, and took a task sheet that Debbie had printed out from the HOLMES database.

Casting her eyes down the list, she noted the major points the computer system had highlighted and raised her voice over the din.

'Settle down, everyone. Grab a seat wherever you can.'

She spent the first twenty minutes of the briefing bringing the newcomers up to date, the room silent except for the scratching of pens in notebooks or, in Debbie's case, tapping her fingers across her computer keyboard.

'So, next steps,' said Kay. 'Lucas Anderson has

emailed me to confirm the post mortem will be conducted tomorrow afternoon, at which point we'll hopefully have some information we can start to process to ascertain who our victim is. In the meantime, Carys – can you work with Debbie and contact the highways department to find out when that lay-by was last cleared? I'm presuming they must have some sort of roster for doing that, especially during the summer months.'

'Guv.' Carys bowed her head, her pen flying across the page of her notebook.

'Barnes, Gavin – I'd like you to liaise with uniform to go through the statements taken from local residents to find out which of those have security cameras installed at their properties. It looks like there are a few people in that area who run businesses from home, too, so I'm hopeful they're security conscious enough to have some sort of external monitoring system that might face the road. If anyone strikes you as being of particular interest, let me know straight away – we'll see if we can start collecting footage this afternoon.'

'Will do.' Gavin leaned across to Barnes and muttered under his breath, the older detective nodding before turning his attention back to Kay.

While Kay reeled off the rest of the day's tasks to

her team, she was struck by how well they had gelled over the past eighteen months.

It worried her, though, that bringing a new detective sergeant into the fray would affect the dynamics she treasured. For all his bluster, Barnes was the glue within the team and both Gavin and Carys were showing a lot of potential to advance in their careers with Kent Police.

She sighed inwardly as she listened to Sergeant Hughes read out the roster he'd drawn up to ensure the investigation was well-manned, and realised that juggling personnel was one more of the management duties she'd unwittingly signed up for when accepting her promotion to detective inspector.

How on earth was she supposed to run an investigation while introducing an unknown element into the group and keep the balance?

SEVEN

Kay leafed through the three-page document in her hands, the evenly spaced text blurring as she struggled to concentrate.

While the incident room buzzed with the rigour of a team of officers making phone calls, shouting to each other across the room and two photocopying machines rumbling non-stop in the far corner, Kay held her head in her hands and tried to concentrate on the pile of résumés the personnel department had emailed to her.

Sharp had insisted she be involved in the interview and selection process for their new detective sergeant, and she had a sudden urge to throw the whole lot on the floor in frustration.

'Oh, for goodness sakes, Ian – listen to this one.

"Demonstrates a high capability of maintaining office records." So, basically, he's good at updating HOLMES. Surely that goes without saying? I mean, if he can't use the system properly he wouldn't be applying for the position, right?'

'Bet he can't type, either,' said Barnes, grinning.

'Never again,' said Kay, dumping the résumé onto a growing pile at her elbow. 'Not now I've got you up to speed.'

A serious expression flitted across Barnes's face. 'Is DCI Larch definitely not coming back, then?'

She shook her head and dropped the pile of documentation into a tray on the corner of her desk. 'No – he won't be back. Sharp said that after his wife died, Larch decided that he'd had enough, and opted to take early retirement. I think he's planning to move back to the Midlands to be closer to his youngest daughter.'

'So, Sharp will be top dog permanently.'

'Guess so.'

'That's good. He can be abrupt, but at least you know where you stand with him.'

Kay held up her hand as her desk phone trilled.

'Hello?'

'DI Hunter?'

'Yes?'

'It's Helen Box.'

Kay frowned, and wracked her memory for the name, but none came to her. 'I'm sorry – do we know each other?'

'I'm the local councillor for Boughton Monchelsea. What are you doing about finding that killer?'

'Ms Box—'

'It's Mrs. I've had phone call after phone call for the past twenty-four hours from my constituents, all worried for their safety. What do I tell them, hmm?'

'Mrs Box, we're at the beginning of our investigation and as you'll appreciate, the timing is critical. We've put out a statement to the media which you're welcome to refer your constituents to. If you let me have a note of your email address, I'll ask our media liaison officer to send you a copy. As and when we have more information to hand that we can share with the public, we'll do so.'

'That's not good enough. Have you arrested anyone yet? I can't have people terrified for their lives.'

Kay glanced across the desk, and saw Barnes watching her, his eyebrow raised. She spun her forefinger in the air, at which point he cupped his hands around his mouth and called out to her.

'Inspector Hunter, there's an urgent phone call for you.'

Kay winked, then turned her attention back to Box. 'I'm sorry, Mrs Box – an emergency has come up that I have to deal with. Rest assured, I'll call you when I have some news.'

She replaced the receiver in the cradle with a sigh. 'I owe you one, Ian.'

He grinned. 'There's always one pain in the—'

'Guv?'

Kay glanced over her shoulder at Gavin's voice. 'What's up?'

The younger detective crossed to them, his mobile phone in his hand. 'I've been speaking with a bloke called David Carter, lives about half a mile up the road from the lay-by. Uniform tried to interview him yesterday but he was away for the weekend. Reckons he might have something on his security camera footage that'll help us.'

'Are you on your way over there?'

'Yes. Do you want to—'

Kay shoved back her chair and swept her mobile phone into her bag. 'Yes, I do. Barnes – hold the fort. I'll be back in time for the briefing.'

'Okay. What about the candidates?' He glanced at the pile of applications in her tray.

She grimaced. 'The ones in there can go in the bin, but there are seven in that folder that might be worth interviewing. I'll give Sharp a call on the way over to Boughton Monchelsea so he can organise them with personnel.'

———

'SO, can I ask how you're finding the new role?'

Gavin swung the car out into Palace Avenue and accelerated to beat a traffic light that was already amber.

Kay let the minor infringement pass without comment and sighed. 'Well, put it this way, Gav. Don't rush up the career ladder, okay?'

He laughed. 'Point taken.'

'How are you getting on?'

'It's been a slow morning going through all the witness statements, but we're getting there. Hopefully this bloke might provide us with a nudge in the right direction.'

'What does he do?'

'Semi-retired now. Used to work for one of the large petroleum companies, travelling around the world to do their IT systems. Does a bit of consulting here and there these days.'

Kay plucked her phone from her bag and thumbed through her emails, before deciding all the messages could wait until her return to the police station and settling in for the short ride.

The Kentish countryside had exploded with colour during the first week of June, and now that summer was well underway it would only be a matter of weeks before the long school holiday break began and the roads would become even more congested.

She and Adam had planned to take a last-minute break to the Continent before the prices shot up as the schools emptied – they'd been discussing potential destinations when Sharp had called her on Sunday, and so she resigned herself to the fact it'd be September before they'd get away.

She set her jaw and turned her attention back to the road as Gavin slowed the car and indicated left as he drew up to a set of metal gates.

A voice intercom had been fixed to the right-hand rendered pillar, and while Gavin announced their arrival, she peered up at the house beyond.

Many of the houses along the lane were older buildings that had been renovated over time. David Carter's home stood out from the rest as it was only a few years old, and modern in design.

Box-like appendages stuck out from the top left-hand side of the house, while a long rectangular window began to the right of the front door and ran the length of the building, the interior hidden behind darkened privacy glass.

Gavin released the handbrake and edged the car forward as the gates opened inwards, and Kay marvelled at the landscaping that hugged the asphalt driveway, while a mixture of mature trees shielded the building from its neighbours.

'Wow. This is like something off that television programme with all the flash houses,' she said.

'I'd hate to think how much it cost.'

'IT consulting must be doing all right.'

The front door opened as Gavin eased the car to a halt and Kay climbed out.

David Carter stood on the step, his grey hair cut medium length, his blue eyes expectant. He wore a pale blue shirt over cream-coloured trousers and held out his hand as they approached.

'I hope this isn't a waste of time, detectives, but I thought I should phone you when I saw the news.'

'We appreciate it,' said Kay, stepping over the threshold and wiping her feet on a mat that stretched across a polished concrete floor. 'We'd rather hear from people who think they might have something for us than be left wondering.'

He closed the door after Gavin and beckoned to them.

'My office is upstairs. Don't worry about your shoes. Come on up.'

He led the way across a hallway and up a staircase that was hugged on either side by bright red walls interspersed with alcoves. In each, a sculpture or piece of high end bric-à-brac sat positioned under a spotlight, and Kay took her time to admire the pieces as she followed Carter and Gavin.

At the top, the IT consultant stood to one side, and Kay found herself in an open plan office, the likes of which she'd never seen before.

She realised she was standing at the edge of the box-shaped structures she'd seen from the driveway, which on the inside created a series of large alcoves around a central working area.

In one, a hammock hung from the ceiling with a tall lamp to one side for reading. In another, a series of bookshelves had been fixed so each would slide out towards the room, an index system inscribed on the end so Carter could see at a glance what was inside.

Along the left-hand wall, a floor–to-ceiling window had been set into each of the alcoves, sending light streaming into the workplace.

'This is amazing,' she managed.

Carter grinned. 'I'd always wanted a working space like this when I was travelling around the world. When I started my own business, I thought "why not?" Some might say it's pretentious, but I like it.' He gestured towards the desk. 'I've got the security footage on my laptop here. I realise you'll want all of the recordings, but I couldn't resist taking a look myself. I know most of my neighbours' vehicles, see? But I haven't spotted this one before, which is why I called you.'

They followed him and waited while he logged in and brought up the imagery on screen.

Kay leaned closer as the pictures sprung to life when he pressed another key.

The summer nights had been clear with a moon halfway through its cycle, and the lane outside Carter's house had been bathed in a cool blue light at the time of the recording.

'When was this taken?'

'This is from five nights ago. Each film is saved in two-hour blocks,' he said. 'We're about fifty-five minutes into this one. Here we go.'

He tapped the screen as a pale-coloured pickup truck shot past the camera.

'Can you slow down the footage?' said Gavin.

'Sure.'

Carter reached out and tapped on the keyboard, resetting the recording to the point before the vehicle appeared, and then hit the "play" button once more.

This time, the pickup crawled past, and Kay narrowed her eyes.

'Any idea what make that is, Gav?'

'Not from here, but it's ancient – the shape is all wrong for any current makes or models. I reckon it has to be about twenty years old. And, even if we take a copy of this to Grey and his digital forensics team, it's not going to be of much use to us yet. Look.'

Kay swore under her breath.

'It's had its number plate removed, dammit.'

EIGHT

Kay pushed through the front door to her home and stumbled over the threshold, fatigue sweeping over her.

She hadn't even seen Adam that morning; he had left before daybreak after a phone call from a farmer out beyond Hacking who bred alpacas.

Kay could hear him in the kitchen now, the beat of a knife on the chopping board and the pungent aroma of onion tickling her senses as she kicked off her shoes and dumped her bag on the bottom stair tread.

She padded in bare feet along the hallway and tied her hair back into a ponytail before entering the kitchen and sliding onto one of the stools next to the worktop.

Adam turned away from the cooker hob and

smiled, a wooden spoon in his hand as he stirred the beginnings of a spaghetti Bolognese.

She cast her eyes around the kitchen, confused.

'What's wrong?' he said.

'No furry visitors?'

He grinned. 'I've got something special lined up for you, but you have to wait.'

'Oh no. What? Please tell me it's not another snake.'

'I wouldn't do that to you again,' he said. He balanced the spoon on the handle of the saucepan, then opened the refrigerator and pulled out a bottle of white wine before wandering over to the worktop where she sat.

Kay slid two empty wine glasses towards him and waited while he poured a generous measure into each.

'You'd better not,' she said, clinking her glass against his.

He winked, took a sip from his wine then moved back to the hob. 'What time are Barnes and Pia getting here tomorrow night?'

'I would imagine Barnes and I won't finish until at least half past six, so half seven perhaps?'

'Good – that gives me plenty of time to prepare for the barbecue.'

Kay listened as Adam described his plans for

what to cook the next night including locally sourced meat. He went out of his way to support others who were trying to keep old traditions alive, many of whom he met while he was doing his rounds of the Kentish farms near Maidstone.

'Do you need me to pick up anything on the way home?' she said, taking another sip of wine and setting down her glass on the worktop.

'No, you're fine – I picked up as much as I could today, and I've got Scott helping in surgery tomorrow. He's offered to take on any emergencies that crop up tomorrow night, so I can relax for a bit.'

'He seems to be settling in well.'

'He is – and very business savvy for his age, too.'

Scott Mildenhall had joined the practice eight months ago after Adam had managed to persuade him to leave the smaller clinic he'd been working at near Paddock Wood. With the promise of opportunities to broaden his horizons and work with bigger animals such as cattle and racehorses, Scott hadn't needed much persuading. Kay had only met him once, but the thickset thirty-something had been friendly and keen to contribute to the success of the clinic, and Adam had grown to rely on him.

'Where do you want to eat, in here or outside?' said Kay.

Adam left the hob and moved to the kitchen window, craning his neck. 'In here, I reckon. They were forecasting a shower tonight. We should be okay for the barbecue tomorrow, though.'

'Sounds good.'

Kay slipped from the bar stool and opened a drawer, collecting cutlery and placing it on the worktop before retrieving the wine bottle and topping up their glasses while Adam dished out spaghetti and sauce onto two square plates. He'd already grated a large pyramid-shaped pile of Parmesan cheese and as Kay sprinkled a generous amount over her dinner, her stomach rumbled loudly.

'Good timing,' said Adam, grinning. 'Guess you didn't get time to eat today?'

She shook her head. 'I'm starving.'

'Well, don't stand on ceremony – get stuck in before you pass out.'

They fell silent as they ate, and Kay savoured every mouthful. She was lucky that Adam enjoyed cooking so much – her own attempts were limited to meals she'd prepared when still a student at university, and after one episode when Adam had witnessed her nearly remove her own thumb with a vegetable knife, she'd been relegated to chief dishwasher stacker.

As she lowered her fork and spoon to her plate for the last time, her mobile phone started to ring.

'Damn,' she muttered, and hurried out to the hallway to retrieve it from her bag.

Carys's number appeared on the display.

'Hey – what's up?'

'Switch the television on,' said the young detective. 'You're not going to believe this.'

Kay frowned, then shrugged at Adam who'd appeared at the kitchen door, both glasses of wine in his hands and a quizzical expression on his face.

'Carys says to put the television on.'

'The news finished ten minutes ago.'

'I don't know why, then – she said to switch it on.'

He gestured towards the living room door with the glasses. 'Lead the way.'

Kay put her phone to her ear once more and made her way through to the living room, picking up the remote control from the coffee table as she sat down and aiming it at the television.

'What's going on, Carys?'

'Change to the local channel, not the BBC.'

Kay did as she was told, then swore profusely, her words echoed by Adam a split second later.

On screen, Suzie Chambers presided over a small

group of guests lined up on a bright red sofa, her face earnest as she spoke to the camera.

'One of our local councillors, Mrs Helen Box, is here to talk about the effect this horrifying find has had on her local constituency, and to her left, we welcome Stephen Mannering, spokesman for the Friends of the Parish group who have offered support to anyone affected by these terrible events.'

Kay groaned, dropped the remote onto the table in front of her, and took the glass Adam handed to her as he perched on the arm of the sofa.

'How did you know?' she said to Carys as she watched the proceedings on the television.

'A mate of mine called me. Apparently, the programme is a new weekly current affairs thing the broadcaster is testing. Suzie's role as presenter was kept under wraps for the past few months. First thing anyone knew about it was when they announced it after the six o'clock news and did a short promotional clip with Suzie saying she had an exclusive about the remains found yesterday. They ran the sports headlines, then cut straight into this.'

She fell silent as the camera panned in on the local councillor's face as Suzie questioned her about her concerns.

'Well, I certainly think the police could be more

cooperative with information being presented to the public,' the woman sniffed. 'After all, we have a duty of care to residents in the area.'

'You don't think what has been reported by the media so far is of assistance?' said Suzie, crossing her legs and leaning forward.

'I think the media are doing the best they can with the information they've got,' said Helen Box. 'What I'm saying is that there must be more they can tell local leaders, even if they're not ready to share that information with the general public.'

'I knew Box would cause trouble after I spoke with her earlier,' said Kay.

'Don't worry about it,' said Carys. 'She's out to make a name for herself before the next by-election. She knows you can't give her any more information than we already have. She was fishing, that's all.'

Kay leaned back against the cushions. 'I wonder what Suzie's game is? Box and Mannering aren't exactly exclusives, are they?'

They both fell silent as Suzie thanked her two guests, then faced the camera, which zoomed in on her perfectly made-up face.

Her expression turned serious as she spoke, her eyes conveying compassion and concern.

'Great actress,' said Carys.

'Shh.'

'Of course, any discovery of this gruesome nature is both shocking and traumatic for the members of the public involved,' said Suzie, her voice betraying her excitement. 'My next guest knows full well the emotional and physical impact such an experience can have, as he was present when his friend found the remains yesterday. Please welcome Paul Banks.'

Kay choked on her wine. 'Oh, bloody hell.'

NINE

Kay paced the floor in front of the whiteboard as the investigation team settled into their seats the next morning and called them to attention the moment the last person sat.

'So, by now I'm assuming you've all heard about one of our witnesses' brief foray into prime-time television.'

A murmur of discontent carried through the room.

'DCI Sharp and the media liaison team are currently meeting with Suzie Chambers and her producer and will be reminding them of their obligations in relation to responsible reporting in future. Given that they've caused irreparable damage to our investigation by interviewing Paul Banks, I have to say I'm glad I'm not at the receiving end of that conversation. In the meantime, Barnes – I want you to contact the other cyclists in the group, especially Lee Temple, and remind them of their obligations in relation to keeping quiet about what they found. You know the drill – make sure they do.'

'Guv.'

Kay tapped a photograph on the whiteboard that had been taken from the security footage on David Carter's computer. 'Piper – let's have an update from you about the video we obtained, please.'

'I've spoken with Andy Grey over at the digital forensics unit,' said Gavin as he moved to the side of the room and turned to face his colleagues. 'He's currently working on enhancing what David Carter gave us to see if he can get a clearer picture of the driver's face or anything that will help us trace the vehicle. I've requested he gives me a call the moment he finds anything to tie that pickup truck to the amputated foot that was found.'

'What about other vehicles passing by?' said Carys. 'Could it have been a different one?'

Gavin shook his head. 'I've been working with Debbie and some of the other uniformed staff to go through all the footage for the ten days leading up to the discovery. Nothing passes on that side of the road that could be construed as a suspect vehicle. No vehicles slow down going past Carter's house, so no-one stopped there and the others are registered with neighbouring properties.'

'Are we sure the foot came from a vehicle, instead of being dumped there by a pedestrian?' said an officer towards the back of the room.

'It's a point worth bearing in mind,' said Kay. 'At the moment, this vehicle is our priority though. If any of you obtain information that could mean a pedestrian was responsible through your enquiries, let Barnes or myself know immediately.'

A murmur swept through the room.

'I'll be working with Maidstone Borough Council to obtain CCTV footage for the area, too,' said Gavin. 'We'll try to trace the vehicle's movements prior to it being spotted on Carter's camera. Maybe that way, we can find out where it was going, or where it came from.'

'Good,' said Kay. 'Speaking of the Borough Council, Carys – did you manage to set up a meeting to speak with their waste team?'

'We're booked in for two o'clock,' said Carys. 'I thought you might like to attend. I'm seeing someone called Robert Wilson.'

'Thanks. Barnes – can you collate from uniform what information they've got on record so far with regard to local businesses? We're looking for anyone out of the way who might have access to the sort of tools it'd take to separate that foot from the rest of our victim's body.'

'Will do.'

'Does anyone have any questions, or are you all clear on today's priorities?'

When no-one spoke up, Kay ended the briefing and wound her way through the room to her desk.

She sank into her chair and eyed the new emails from the personnel department that had appeared in her absence, then glanced longingly at the clock above the photocopier.

Two o'clock couldn't come soon enough.

CARYS LED the way from the incident room to the car park, catching the set of keys that Sergeant Hughes tossed to her as they passed the front desk, and calling her thanks over her shoulder as she and Kay pushed through the rear doors of the police station.

'Which one?'

'The one with air conditioning.' Carys grinned

and headed towards a pale blue four-door vehicle at the outer fringes of the car park.

'Hughes must be in a good mood, taking pity on us like that.'

'I bought him an iced coffee and a pastry this morning.'

'Devious. Nice work.'

The Borough Council offices where they were headed was only a short distance as the crow flies from the police station, but due to roadworks and a convoluted diversion past the grammar school it took Carys over half an hour to reach the depot at Parkwood.

They hurried towards the front doors of the low-slung building at five minutes to the hour.

A blast of cold air conditioning welcomed Kay as she pushed her way through into the reception area and made her way over to the desk.

The man behind the desk raised his gaze as she approached, and she noticed he had the unfortunate habit of pushing his glasses up his nose with his middle finger. She wondered how many visitors had taken the gesture the wrong way.

'Can I help you?' he said, his tone friendly enough.

Kay introduced herself and Carys. 'We're here to

meet with Robert Wilson.'

'Oh, right. No problem. Sign in here, and I'll let him know you've arrived.'

'Thanks.'

She turned away from the desk and tried not to pace the floor as they waited. Thankfully, Wilson appeared moments later, his hand outstretched, a folder under his other arm.

'Detectives, good afternoon. Come on through – there's a meeting room we can use that'll give us a bit of privacy.' He gestured to an open doorway next to the reception desk.

Kay followed in his wake, his long strides powering him ahead of the two police officers.

He guided them along a corridor that ran the length of the building. At the far end, he turned right and they entered a windowless conference room.

Wilson flipped light switches next to the door, then closed it and indicated the seats around the large oval table in the centre before pushing his fringe from his eyes. 'Please, have a seat. Can I get you some water or anything?'

'We're fine, thanks.'

'I guess you're here about the human remains that were found on Sunday.' His green eyes sparkled.

Kay noticed the tell-tale sign of someone who

enjoyed the sensationalism of reports such as Suzie Chambers' and who was eager to learn more.

He'd be disappointed.

She folded her hands on the table and made sure Carys was ready to take notes before she began.

'Mr Wilson, can you tell me when that lay-by was last cleaned by your team?'

'Um, it would have been five weeks ago, because it was due to be done again this Friday.' He shuddered. 'Horrible. I can't imagine what it was like for that cyclist and his friends.'

'Five weeks?'

'Yes, that's the cycle. The council's responsible for all the street cleaning in the area as well as bus shelters, country roads, and lay-bys.'

'And you're sure that every lay-by is checked?'

'We have key performance indicators for each member of our personnel. If they weren't doing their job properly, the public would let us know, I can assure you.'

He chuckled and leaned back in his seat.

'We'll need the names of the cleaning team.'

His brow puckered. 'Oh, I see. That might be a bit tricky, as sometimes we use temporary staff to complement our own contingent of workers.'

'Do those temporary staff have performance

reviews as well?'

'No, we bring them in as and when needed.'

'So, if they were responsible for that route five weeks ago, they might have missed that lay-by and you wouldn't know.'

'Like I said, we usually hear from the public if there's litter lying around that hasn't been dealt with.'

'What if no-one reported it?'

His jaw set, and he swallowed before answering. 'Then I guess it would be done on the next five-week cycle.'

'Do you have records of those permanent and temporary staff responsible for that route?'

'Yes, of course – it'll just take time.'

'Is there someone here who can let us have that information this afternoon? As you'll appreciate, this is an important investigation and we're rather keen to catch the person who did this.'

Wilson's cheeks flamed crimson, and he rose from his seat. 'Hang on. I'll see what I can do.'

As he left the room, Kay turned to Carys and rolled her eyes.

'You'd have thought he'd have organised that before we got here.'

'I did ask.' Carys sighed. 'Some people have no sense of urgency, do they?'

TEN

Kay waited beside Barnes as he pressed the button on the intercom to the right-hand side of the glass doors and announced their arrival to the staff at the mortuary.

She could have tasked Gavin or Carys to go with him, but she still craved direct action over paperwork and was glad of the excuse to escape from the incident room for a while. Besides, they were under-staffed, and if a detective inspector chose to roll up her sleeves to help out, no-one was complaining.

Sharp had worn a harried expression upon his return from a meeting at headquarters, and she knew he was thinking the same as the rest of them – what if this slaying wasn't a one-off?

Her thoughts were interrupted at the sound of the locking mechanism being released. Barnes opened the door and gestured to her to follow him over the threshold.

A gangly twenty-something held out his hand, his blue eyes so stark against his pale skin and dark brown hair that Kay wondered if he wore special contact lenses.

'I'm Simon Winter. Lucas's new assistant.'

Kay and Barnes introduced themselves, then followed Simon along the corridor to the office. They waited while he retrieved a folder from the desk and flipped it open.

'You're here for the post mortem on the foot that was found?'

'That's right.'

'Okay, well I'll be assisting Lucas today.' He glanced up at the clock on the wall. 'He's finishing off another PM at the moment, but if you'd like to come this way, I'll sort you out with some coveralls. Do you want a tea or coffee or anything?'

Both detectives shook their heads.

Kay would never get used to the normality that Lucas and his staff conveyed at the morgue – the idea of eating or drinking anywhere near a dead body filled her with revulsion.

Simon led them from the office to the changing rooms. 'You'll find the coveralls sealed in packets on the shelves just inside the doors. There are lockers there for your belongings, and you can put the coveralls in the biohazard bins provided when we're finished.' He jerked his thumb over his shoulder. 'I'll meet you inside. It's the door on the right, there.'

Fifteen minutes later, Kay shuffled her feet, and tried to ignore the itching at the back of her neck caused by an errant label from the disposable coveralls she wore.

Next to her, Barnes grumbled under his breath and checked his watch.

'I thought he said he was starting this at half past two.'

'It's been busy this week,' said Simon. 'There were a couple of nasty accidents on the M20 on Sunday on top of our current workload – tourists from the Continent. Seems they forgot what side of the road they were supposed to be driving on.'

Kay grimaced. The summer months always brought an influx of travellers from Europe, which was a boon for the tourism industry but brought a high risk of accident and injury on the busy roads. And this was before the UK schools closed for the summer holidays.

The door behind her opened and Lucas appeared, snapping a fresh pair of gloves onto his hands. One look at his harried face put paid to any thoughts of a flippant remark, and even Barnes held his tongue.

'Sorry, Kay, Ian. Nasty one next door – two young children. House fire at the weekend over at Leybourne.'

He sighed, then turned his attention to the object Simon had prepared in the middle of the examination table. He cocked an eyebrow.

'You seem to have a habit of bringing me body parts with the rest of their owner missing, Hunter.'

The bleak mood lifted a little, and Kay and Barnes joined him at the table.

'I don't know about you, but I'm finding this easier to deal with than a decapitated head,' she said.

Lucas gestured to Simon, who reached up and pulled a toggle on the end of a cord, and a bright light flickered on above their heads and illuminated the severed foot.

The pathologist provided a running commentary as he worked, dictating into a microphone clipped to the lapel of his overalls while Simon handed him various surgical instruments.

Kay knew from experience that although his

report would be thorough, it was often best to attend the post mortem so that she could have the opportunity to ask questions as they arose, rather than wait for a returned phone call or email to clarify something that might be urgent.

The pathologist's examination was over within thirty minutes. He switched off his microphone and turned to Kay and Barnes.

'All right, there's not much to go on, but your victim was certainly dead when his foot was removed. He had suffered an injury to his big toe within recent months and appears to have an ongoing issue with it, here. I've removed a dressing that had been applied professionally.'

Kay peered across to where he indicated and saw an area of broken skin.

'So, we start with local podiatrists, hospitals, that sort of thing,' said Barnes.

'That's our best bet. See if anyone has missed an appointment recently.' Kay glanced across the table at Lucas. 'You think he would have been having regular treatment for this?'

Lucas nodded. 'That would have been painful to walk on. In fact, I'd go so far as to suggest he was already overdue for an appointment.'

'What about the cutting method used? To separate the foot from the leg, I mean.'

'Well, it's not a professional job, but that doesn't mean you should rule out anyone in the medical profession – I simply mean that a surgical implement wasn't used. You're looking for something crude, probably blunt, too.' He used his little finger to indicate the stump. 'Notwithstanding the damage caused by wildlife before this was discovered, the skin and muscle has been torn – probably by back-and-forth movement, such as with a saw – and you can see here the grooves made in the bone from that instrument. We'll run some more tests to see if we can pinpoint an exact type.'

Kay straightened. 'Okay, let's get back to the station. We've already got people reviewing the missing persons database. If no-one has been reported as missing an appointment, then we'll start with local clinics and widen the search if we need to. How old is it? I mean, how long since it had been—'

'—separated from its owner? A couple of days, no more,' said Lucas. 'Which of course begs the question – where's the rest of him?'

'That's what worries us,' said Barnes. 'Uniform have done a search of the lay-by, the road, the verge opposite, and the hedgerows. They haven't found anything.'

Kay groaned. 'This was never going to be easy, was it?'

'We haven't got a leg to stand on,' said Barnes, then yelped as she slapped his arm.

ELEVEN

Later that day, Kay forced a smile while she rose from her seat and held out her hand to the pock-marked faced candidate once he'd gathered up his notes and jacket.

'We'll be in touch,' she said, and guided him towards the door, indicating he should go on without her.

After making sure he was out of earshot, she turned to Sharp. 'You'd have thought if he'd applied to be transferred here, he'd have done some bloody homework about the place,' she hissed.

He rolled his eyes in answer and waved her out of the room.

She caught up with the candidate, and once she'd seen him out through the reception area, she turned to

Sergeant Hughes behind the desk. 'Where's our next one?'

He jerked his head at a meeting room off to the side. 'In there. You look like you could do with a drink.'

'I've already had two coffees.'

'I meant alcoholic.'

She grinned. 'Later, Hughes.'

He winked, then she straightened her jacket and opened the door to the meeting room.

A man stopped pacing the room as she entered and spun around.

His short brown hair framed a round face that beamed at her, his hands dropping from the tie he had been adjusting.

'Brendan Rhodes?'

'Detective Inspector Hunter, it's an honour to meet you in person.' Rhodes advanced towards her so fast, Kay took a step back as her mouth dropped open.

He paused, a troubled expression crossing his face, then stuck out his hand.

'Sorry – it's just that I read about your case against Jozef Demiri last year. It was so inspiring.'

She narrowed her eyes. 'Shall we? DCI Sharp is waiting for us.'

'Of course, of course.'

Kay held open the door for him, then used her swipe card to let him through the security barrier next to the desk, ignoring the grin plastered across Hughes's face.

Sharp greeted Rhodes at the door to the interview room and raised a quizzical eyebrow at her.

She shook her head and lowered herself into the chair next to his, waited until the two men had settled and cleared her throat.

'Brendan, you've requested a transfer from East Sussex to take up the position of detective sergeant with Kent Police here in Maidstone. Can you tell us why?'

Rhodes shuffled in his seat, a faint blush appearing on his neck that slowly worked its way towards his cheeks.

'I'm ready for a new challenge, and I feel that Kent offers more opportunities for results-driven detective work than I might see in Hastings.'

Kay bit down hard on her lip to stop herself from smiling at the prepared answer and gestured to Sharp to intervene.

'I'm sure East Sussex has its fair share of challenges,' he said. 'What have some of your recent successes included?'

As Kay listened to Rhodes answering each question posed, the monotony of his voice distracted her and she found her thoughts returning to the investigation continuing without her in the room above.

She itched to be there with her colleagues, delving into the information they'd collated to date, and dealing with the numerous decisions to be fielded and actions every few minutes.

She was jerked back to the interview at the sound of her name.

'—Hunter. It'd be an honour and a real career highlight to work with you. After all, you were so brave to take on Jozef Demiri.'

Sharp managed to disguise his burst of laughter with a fake sneeze.

Kay glared at him before turning her attention to the candidate.

'I'm not sure what rumours you've been listening to, Mr Rhodes, but the apprehension of Jozef Demiri was a team effort following an exhaustive investigation. I'm afraid Kent Police, as well as many other forces, takes a rather dim view of individuals seeking recognition to further their own careers.'

Rhodes blushed and, suitably chastened, answered the rest of the prepared questions with an intensity borne of evident embarrassment.

Minutes later, Kay closed the file in front of her as

Sharp stood and thanked Rhodes before leading him out to the reception area, then checked her watch.

The investigative team would still be upstairs, and she wanted to make sure she was in attendance for the briefing. Barnes was more than capable, but she knew from first-hand experience that some of the best theories could be shared amongst the group at that time, and she wanted to be present to galvanise them into action if required.

Footsteps reached her ears as Sharp returned.

He patted her shoulder as he passed, then perched on the desk facing her, the corner of his mouth twitching.

'What do you think of your one-man fan club?'

'It's not funny. I can't believe he applied for the job, just so he could tell his mates he met me.'

He couldn't contain his mirth any longer and let out a laugh.

'Stop it. Give me some good news, Devon.'

'Personnel have organised another three interviews for tomorrow.'

Kay leaned forward and rested her head on her arms as a groan escaped her lips.

'I'd take a post mortem over this any day.'

TWELVE

The sound of the doorbell cut through Kay's singing midway through the classic Aerosmith track, and she leaned over the worktop and turned down the speakers before wiping her hands on a towel.

Barnes and his partner, Pia McLeod, stood on the doorstep.

'Hey, come on through,' said Kay, and moved to one side. 'Adam's on his way. I'm just making the salads.'

'We brought wine,' said Pia. 'Hope it's okay.'

'If it's white and cold, it'll be absolutely fine,' Kay said with a smile.

She and Adam had first been introduced to Pia a little over a year ago. After Barnes's daughter, Emma, had nagged him about losing weight and had then attacked her father's unfashionable wardrobe with a vengeance, he had starting dating again and it wasn't long before he found love in his life once more.

Smart, funny, and a conveyancing solicitor with a local firm, Pia was a perfect match for Barnes's gruff humour, and the two couples had spent many a time at each other's houses in the months since.

Kay envied the way Pia moved with grace along the hallway on her three-inch high sandals. If she tried to wear anything similar, she'd wreck her ankles within minutes.

Kay followed them through to the kitchen, then picked up a knife and began slicing tomatoes while Barnes and Pia helped themselves, at ease in her home.

Barnes reached out to turn up the speakers a little and grinned as he poured a bottle of beer into a pint glass.

'Still listening to the old stuff?'

'Can't beat it.'

'Do you want me to go and fire up the barbecue?'

'That'd be great, thanks.'

As Barnes took his pint of beer and headed out the back door, Pia joined her at the worktop.

'Anything I can do?'

Kay cast her eyes over the salad ingredients in

front of her. 'Despite what Adam might say about me and kitchens, I think I've got this under control.'

Fifteen minutes later, the three of them were gathered around the teak outdoor table and enjoying the breeze that teased the air.

Kay had her back to the house and savoured the view of the garden – she wasn't naturally green-fingered but did enjoy pottering around the flower bed she'd been working on since the spring.

Barnes had taken charge of the barbecue, and the faint sound of gas hissed on the air.

'Never understood why Adam uses a gas one,' he said, taking a seat next to Pia and clinking his glass against theirs.

'I think he finds it easier to clean compared to the charcoal ones,' said Kay, easing back into her chair.

'It's not the same though. You've got to admit, there's something very summer-like having barbecue smoke wafting across the garden.'

'It's relaxing, too isn't it?' said Pia. 'Takes me back to my childhood.'

'Same here. And, anyway—' Barnes broke off, his mouth dropping open before he recovered. 'What the bloody hell is that?'

A mournful bleat reached Kay's ears, and when

she glanced over her shoulder, she snorted cold beer up her nose.

'Oh, my God,' she said, spluttering. She reached out for a napkin and cleaned up, then turned as Adam appeared on the back step with a tray of meat in his hands.

She pointed at the miniature goat that had burst through the door seconds before. 'What on earth is that doing in our garden?'

Adam put the tray on the table, said a quick hello to Barnes and Pia, then patted his hands on his jeans.

The goat skipped across the lawn to him and butted against his leg while he scratched at its fawn-coloured coat.

'This is Misha.'

'What's she doing here?'

'Keeping the grass down.'

Barnes laughed, and Kay glared at him.

'It's not funny.'

'He's outdone himself this time – admit it.'

She fought to keep a straight face while she took in the wiry-haired animal. Despite her protestations, she had to admit Misha was cute.

When the goat left Adam's side and ambled over to her though, she noticed her limping.

'What's wrong with her?'

'I had to trim her hooves this morning – the rescue centre we sponsor took her in yesterday after her owner said he couldn't look after her anymore, and the procedure has left her a bit sore in her front left foot. I picked her up after I'd been to the butchers on The Green. She'll be fine in a week or so, but I thought she'd be happier here with a bit of company than stuck in a pen at the clinic while she heals up.'

'Aw, poor thing.'

She ignored the laughter from the others as she leaned over and scratched Misha between the ears, and realised she'd enjoy having the animal to stay. She usually did when Adam brought unusual guests home – except for the time he tended a sick snake.

'Will she be safe here?'

'Should be, yes – Ian, if you don't mind I was going to ask if you'd give me a hand making an enclosure for her after we've eaten? I went to the hardware store this morning and got what we'll need.'

'Sure, no problem.'

Kay straightened and noticed the ring of wire fencing Adam had already placed against the far side of the house. She loved the urban foxes that roamed the neighbourhood, but Misha would be no match for them. At least now while she stayed with her and Adam, she'd be safe at night, especially since he had also brought home one of the large crates from the clinic to put in a corner of the makeshift pen.

'Sit down, I'll grab you a beer,' she said, and made her way into the kitchen.

Kay could hear the others making a fuss of the miniature goat as she grabbed more drinks from the refrigerator, and by the time she'd returned to the patio, Adam had clipped Misha's collar onto a long lead that he'd fixed to one of the downpipes on the side of the house.

The goat glared at him, her position now several paces away from the table full of food.

Even Kay had to laugh as she topped up glasses and handed Adam a pint of his favourite real ale.

'She's sulking.'

'She can sulk all she likes. This salad looks fabulous, and she's not getting any.'

A mournful bleat reached their ears.

'I have to say, I'm surprised you didn't postpone this,' said Pia as Adam moved to the barbecue and began setting out the meat to cook. 'Ian said you have a particularly nasty one on your hands at the moment.'

'I nearly did, but then I figured it might be a few weeks before we get together again,' said Kay. 'I imagine we're going to be putting in some long hours for a while now.'

Barnes leaned forward and dropped an olive stone in the ceramic pot in the centre of the table. 'I'd second that. I've been looking forward to this. It was worth it anyway just to see the look on your face, Hunter, when that goat appeared.'

'Very funny.'

THIRTEEN

Geoffrey Cornwell woke early after the promise of a perfect summer's day broke through the cracks in the blinds over the bedroom window an hour before the alarm was due to go off.

He didn't mind; he made a cup of tea for his wife, left it on the bedside table and gave her a gentle nudge to wake her, before making his way downstairs and sitting on the patio with his coffee and the newspaper.

Their dog, a Beagle by the name of Alan – a legacy of when the kids were too young to know any better, and too insistent for him to refuse – sat beside him, lazily snapping at any flies that bothered them.

His shift started at seven o'clock.

Arriving at the disused quarry site, he swiped his

security card across the panel at the gate, guided his car through the gap, and transferred his lunch box and water bottle to the staff room before grabbing the keys for the plant machine he would be operating.

He blinked and used the sleeve of his high visibility long-sleeved shirt to wipe at the sweat that tickled at his brow.

By mid-morning, the temperature was soaring.

Geoffrey adjusted the controls on the excavator and let his mind wander to the darts match he was due to compete in that night. Alan would accompany him, of course. The dog had a penchant for the cheese-flavoured snacks that were sold behind the bar of The Blue Anchor, and only got them when Mary wasn't around to see.

That was still six hours away though, and the day was proving to be a long one.

The air-conditioning in the cab of the excavator had stopped working a couple of months ago, and no-one had worried then – summer was a late arrival to the south of England, and the thought of incurring an unnecessary expense was obviously not at the top of his employers "to do" list at the time.

Now he wished he could strip the shirt off his back.

The cab had small windows on each side, but

these had been designed for adjusting the mirrors, and nothing else. He could only catch a breeze through them when he turned the plant machine to the left before swinging the bucket around and attacking the landfill before him once more.

It wasn't enough.

Running his tongue over parched lips, he manoeuvred the controls over the waste vegetation and soil. He would work another ten minutes, then have a break and wander over to the site office to refill his water bottle.

It was all right for Mary – she worked at one of the local car showrooms in a state-of-the-art office with ducted air conditioning, and often complained that it was too cold. Geoffrey had laughed that morning after she had appeared downstairs with a cardigan draped over her arm, and he wondered how she would cope with the heat in the cab.

She'd probably relish it.

He forced himself to concentrate, the scrape and pull of the bucket across the earth an unsteady rhythm that shook the cab whenever it encountered a rock.

That morning, he had topped up the oil and refuelled the tank with diesel before beginning his shift. In the old days, whoever used the vehicle the day before would ensure the fuel tank was full for the next man's shift but with the rise in theft, his employers' recent stance and change to procedure made sense.

Now, he kept an eye on the machine as it worked, his hands moving automatically on joysticks.

He raised his gaze to where one of the other shift workers operated a second excavator a few hundred metres away.

Each of the machines worked autonomously, its operator burrowing through the waste that couldn't be sent to the incinerator at Allington and converted into energy for the surrounding area.

Their role was to segregate what could be recycled, then bury what was left.

Since he'd starting working at the site two years ago, he and Mary had become increasingly aware of what they purchased – the sheer wastage he encountered every day had shocked him, and he'd been a staunch supporter when his employers had announced they'd be reclaiming more of the green waste the excavator now burrowed through and sell it on for garden mulch.

Geoffrey swung the machine around to the right and angled the bucket at the next pile of tangled branches and soil, and then froze.

Beyond the scratched and dirty front window of the cab, the boom of the excavator hung in the air, waiting for his next manoeuvre.

He didn't move.

Half a metre under the bucket, the churned waste from the local area yawed before him.

And, perched on top of the pile of soil he'd turned, was an object that would be the source of nightmares for weeks, if not months.

He reached out, put the controls into a neutral setting, then switched off the engine and swung open the door.

His legs shook as he lowered himself from the cab, his hands clutching at the safety rails on each side. When he reached the ground, he paused for a moment, his stomach churning.

He swallowed, fighting down the bile that rose in his throat, and glanced towards the exposed ground.

It could have only been there for a few days. His role at the landfill was to sort and transfer incoming waste so that it could be processed by others elsewhere on site, and a new pile was already forming on the other side of the office buildings.

Geoffrey exhaled, set his shoulders, and moved towards it.

He stopped before he reached the bucket of the excavator, his bowels turning to liquid.

Before him, its teeth grinning at his unease and shock, was a scorched and blackened human skull.

FOURTEEN

Kay eyed the black crow as it strutted across the tangle of abandoned tree roots and branches. Every few steps, it paused and stabbed its beak into the decaying vegetation before resuming its path across the edge of the landfill site.

Above her, seagulls spiralled in the air, their cries sending a shiver across her shoulders.

'Here you go.'

She turned and took the plastic coveralls that one of the crime scene investigators held out to her.

'Thanks,' she said, and slipped her feet into the matching booties. She straightened and turned to Barnes who was zipping up coveralls that he'd pulled on over his shirt and trousers. 'Ready?'

'Yes. Let's take a look.'

Kay raised her gaze to the group of people milling about at the far end of the site.

An abandoned excavator towered over Harriet as she issued instructions to her team, while one of her photographers crouched at the foot of the pile of waste that had been encircled with crime scene tape.

She was pleased to see that the first responders had taken the initiative and created a wide perimeter that included the excavator as well as the materials set aside for reclamation. One of the uniformed officers stood at the entry to the crime scene, a clipboard in his hand as he recorded each person's name.

When she and Barnes had arrived at the landfill site, four more uniformed officers were working their way through the roster and interviewing each member of staff as well as their managers.

Due to the dangerous environment and the risk of the mountains of waste collapsing from the number of people in attendance, the owners had insisted on having a maximum of half a dozen of her team within the perimeter at any one time.

It hampered progress, but no-one was going to argue. Safety had to come first.

Kay wrinkled her nose at the stench of rotting vegetation, and envied Harriet's team for their masks. She cursed under her breath as her ankle rolled on the uneven ground, then murmured her thanks as Barnes reached out to steady her.

'I know you're keen to see another dead body, guv, but slow down. It's not going anywhere.'

Kay's lips thinned, and she squinted in the bright sunlight that reflected off the paintwork of the plant machine.

'Where's the driver?'

'He's the bloke over to the left of the excavator – the taller one. Been working here for two years; local to the area. Uniform have taken an initial statement.'

'Okay. Let's see what we've got, and then we'll speak to him.'

She waited at the crime scene tape while Harriet finished speaking to Charlie, her photographer, before turning to the two detectives and waving them over.

Kay scrawled her name across the proffered clipboard, handed it back to the police constable and ducked under the tape.

Harriet gestured to a path that had been pegged out through the crime scene to ensure none of the evidence was contaminated and waited while the two detectives negotiated it to reach her.

'We're going to be here a while, but I can confirm that the skull is human,' she said. 'We've found other remains, too – possibly sections from a femur, three fingers, and a scapula. All have been burned.'

'Do you think it's the same victim as our amputated foot?' said Barnes.

Harriet eyed them both for a moment, then reached out and placed her hand on Kay's arm before steering them further away from the small crowd of curious onlookers.

'We're keeping it quiet at the moment, but it's my belief we have two victims here.'

'Two?' Kay glanced over her shoulder at the exposed soil.

'The femur bone fragments are too small to match the ankle bone we found,' said Harriet. 'Given the amount of damage, I'm going to have to bring in a forensic anthropologist to assist in the identification.'

'I suppose it's going to be a while before we know if these two are connected.'

Harriet scratched at her hair through the plastic hood that covered her head. 'I hate to think that there's more than one person doing this.'

'How on earth will you and Lucas be able to identify them?' said Barnes.

'Burning doesn't destroy all the evidence – we'll still be able to search for signs of DNA from the teeth, for example. With any luck, we might be able to extract enough detail to see if the method of amputation on the other bones was the same as the ankle.'

Kay cast her eyes over the remaining rubbish that had been dumped across the landfill and bit back a sigh.

'I suppose we can't be sure that there isn't more here.'

Harriet pointed to an area that had been cordoned off beyond their position. 'When we got here, we spoke to the owners and ascertained the age of each section of the landfill. Where we are now is the most recent – all of this has been collected within the past two months. Everything over there is more than six months old and is due to be processed over the next few weeks. We plan to work through this more recent stuff over the next few days, and if you need us to – if you think our killer has been active for longer, I mean – then the owner will leave the older rubbish in situ until we've had a chance to go through it.'

'How many people have you got spare to work on this?' said Kay.

'Half a dozen.'

Kay said nothing, but the vastness of the task ahead of Harriet's team was evident.

Harriet led them back to where the skull had been

found, and crouched beside it. She ran her little finger across the base of the bone.

'This looks like a blunt trauma wound. Lucas will be able to tell you a bit more.'

'So, he kills and then cuts up his victim's body.' Kay frowned. 'That's a lot of blood – and wouldn't be easy to do.'

'Not to mention he could be transporting the remains,' said Barnes. 'Maybe that's how he lost the foot.'

'And sets fire to the parts, then dumped them here.' Kay added. 'Hell of a risk moving around so much like that.'

'Kay? Whoever did this didn't expect to be caught,' said Harriet, rising to her feet and brushing her gloved hands on her coveralls.

'You think he's done it before?'

The CSI bit her lip and cast her gaze across the landfill to where a small group of contractors milled about, then back to Kay. 'It's more than my professional opinion will allow me to consider.'

'What's your gut feel?'

Harriet exhaled, her brow creasing. 'I think you need to find him. Before he does this again.'

FIFTEEN

Kay and Barnes left Harriet to supervise her team and stripped out of their coveralls once they reached the perimeter.

A crime scene investigator took the discarded clothing and bundled it into a biohazard bin to avoid contamination, then Kay led the way over to where the excavator driver was standing with a colleague and PC Parker.

The driver appeared to be in his early sixties with a mop of grey-brown hair tousled by the breeze that wafted across the site, and a worried expression on his features.

'Guv? This is Niles Whitman and Geoffrey Corn-well,' said Parker.

'Call me Geoff.' The man stuck his hand out, and

Kay noticed the firm grip as she shook it.

Despite the shock of the find, Cornwell seemed to be holding up well.

She turned to Whitman. 'Is there somewhere we can talk, away from here?'

The site manager jerked his thumb over his shoulder. 'There's a breakout area outside the site office. Deserted at the moment, but it's got tables and chairs. Will that do?'

'Perfect. Lead the way.'

Kay flapped at a fly that buzzed too close to her face and followed Whitman and Cornwell across the pitted and churned up ground, negotiating deep ruts left by the machinery used on the site.

Whitman gestured to a rusted metal table and four camping chairs around it. 'Here we go.'

'Thanks,' said Kay. 'Do you mind if we speak to Geoff alone for a moment, and then we'll catch up with you?'

The manager shrugged. 'No problem.'

Kay watched while he moved to a table at the opposite end of the breakout area, then pulled out a chair and sat beside the excavator driver and waited until Barnes extracted his notebook from his jacket pocket.

'I know you've already given a statement to our

colleagues when they turned up earlier this morning, Geoff, but I wondered if I could ask you a few more questions?'

Cornwell scratched his ear, then dropped his hands into his lap. 'That's fine.'

'Can you tell me in your own words what happened this morning?'

'I started my shift at seven o'clock as usual, I suppose it was about two hours later I was working where the excavator is parked now.'

'Did you see anyone on the landfill before you got to that area?'

'No. When a pile of waste gets to a certain size, we direct the public to dump their green waste on the other side of the site. That would have taken place a week ago. It stops it getting too high, so it doesn't fall on someone and injure them.'

'So, you alternate between the two areas?'

'That's right.'

'Okay. What happened next?'

'I thought it might have been a dog at first. You'd be surprised how many people don't want to pay for pet burial services or can't dig a hole for it at the bottom of the garden because they're renting, so they dump it here.' He shuddered, then swallowed. 'Do you know what happened to him?'

Kay made a slight gesture to Barnes. There was no sense in telling Cornwell that Harriet and her team had discovered more than one body.

'Not yet,' she said. 'But we will. Did you go straight back to the site office?'

'Not straightaway, no. I suppose I was in shock. I switched off the engine – I'm not sure how long I sat there for. In the end, I climbed out the cab to take a closer look. I couldn't believe what I was seeing. When I realised I was right, I ran to the site office and got Ian to phone the police.'

He ran a shaking hand over his mouth. 'I can't believe it. Who would do such a thing?'

Kay looked over the man's shoulder to where Whitman sat and waved him over.

'Geoff, thank you very much for speaking to us. I know you've had one hell of a shock, so I appreciate it. We may be in touch over the next few days with a few more questions, but that will do for now.'

Cornwell nodded, then slapped his hands on his thighs and rose to his feet. 'I suppose I'd better get back to work.'

Whitman stepped forward. 'Geoff, take the rest of the week off. Seriously, after the shock you've had today, it's not a problem. And speak to your GP if you need to, okay?'

The man blinked, then his shoulders relaxed. 'Thanks, Niles. Appreciated.'

'Do you need a lift home?' said Kay.

'No, that's all right – got my wife's car here. I'll be okay.'

She watched as he moved away from the table, his gaze upon the abandoned machinery, then turned and shielded her eyes from the sunlight that bounced off the windscreen of another excavator. She peered at the towering collection of vegetation and other green waste it ploughed through.

'What happens to all of this, Mr Whitman?'

'The excavator operators segregate out the smaller materials for recycling to start off with, then the bigger pieces are broken up and processed.' Whitman pointed across the site. 'The small stuff is put through those large wood chippers and sold back to the public and the local borough councils as bark chippings for ornamental landscaping.'

'Wood chippers? Kay turned and caught Barnes raising an eyebrow at her.

'When were those last operational?' he said to Whitman.

The man paled. 'About four days ago. You don't think—'

He broke off and peered over to where the other

excavator moved back and forth, shovelling green waste towards an increasing pile, close to one of the temporary buildings.

'I need you to halt operations over there until our CSIs have processed what you've sorted so far,' said Kay.

Fortunately the site manager didn't argue, pulled a radio from his belt, and relayed the message.

A crackle of static preceded the machine's engine being halted, and a moment later the operator climbed from the cab, raising his hand in their direction.

Whitman turned to Kay. 'Is there anything else you need?'

'I don't suppose you keep a record of who brings recycling here to be disposed?'

He shook his head. 'No, but we have a camera at the gates into the compound that photographs vehicle licence plates as they enter. Will that help?'

'We'll take it, thanks,' said Kay. 'We're going to need a full list of names for people that work here, as well as any contractors you use from time to time.'

A cloud passed across his features. 'The people that work here are trustworthy, detective.'

'I'm sure they are, but it's routine for us to check every angle, not to mention one of your employees may have seen some suspicious activity.' Her gaze returned to the CSIs as they worked methodically across the swollen ground before them, marking out their progress as each new find was uncovered. 'We have to find who did this.'

Chastened, the man shrugged his shoulders. 'Okay. I'll have one of the girls in the office email them to you.'

'Thanks,' said Kay, and handed him her business card before calling over to Parker. 'One of my officers will accompany you back to the office so he can take a copy of your security camera footage as well.'

Whitman turned away and trudged across the churned earth towards the row of temporary cabins on the outer fringes of the site, his mobile phone to his ear, while Parker hurried after him.

'What do you think?' said Barnes.

'I think Harriet's right. Whoever did this has had practice. How the hell has he stayed hidden, Ian?'

'Luck,' said Barnes. 'Sometimes, that's all it takes.'

Kay wrinkled her nose at the stench of rotting vegetation as she ran her eyes over the piles of rubbish and tried to ignore the sinking sensation in her heart.

'I hate to think how many more victims there are out there.'

SIXTEEN

Barnes removed his tie, folded it, then tossed it onto his desk before threading his way between the assembled officers.

Kay moved to one side as he joined her, and he gave her a quick nod.

'Thanks, guv. Right, everyone. Carys has confirmed we've got a list of personnel and contractor names from the Borough Council, but all of those check out. In the meantime, CCTV footage came through from the landfill site office three hours ago. PC Aaron Stewart and his colleagues from uniform have helped us go through it all, concentrating on drop-offs made in the seven days leading up to the discovery.'

He paused while Gavin moved to the door and

flicked the light switches to one side of it, dropping the incident room into a false twilight. The overhead projector whirred to life, and an image appeared on the plain wall beside the whiteboard. Barnes aimed the remote at it, and the image played through the sequence.

'The quality is shoddy, and the camera to the rear of the building doesn't work at all,' he said. 'However, we have got this.'

He paused the recording as a pale-coloured pickup truck drew up to the gates.

'Is that the same vehicle?' said Carys, leaning forward on her chair.

'We think so.'

'It's got licence plates,' said Kay.

Barnes nodded. 'It has, and we've already run them through the national police computer. They were stolen off a Ford Mondeo parked at the Ashford retail outlet last month.'

A collective groan filled the room.

'What, so he puts on stolen plates to dump the body parts?' said Gavin. 'Can we get a photo of his face from this?'

'Unfortunately, no. He's obviously familiar with the place, because he goes out of his way to avoid his face being seen. He's been here before.'

'Do any of Whitman's employees or contractors recognise the vehicle?' said Kay as she perched on Debbie's desk.

'No – which makes me think it's stolen, too,' said Barnes, 'especially as we have it on David Carter's security footage with no licence plates at all.'

'Hell of a risk driving around with no plates on until he got to the landfill site,' said Carys.

'He probably kept to the back roads,' said Gavin. 'Plenty of places to stay out of the way until he could dump the body parts.'

'I'm not sure,' said Kay. 'This vehicle disappeared for two whole days between Carter's cameras and these. So, where did he go?'

'And where did he hide the body parts?' said Barnes. He waved to Gavin to switch the lights back on and handed the briefing back to Kay as the beam from the overhead projector dimmed.

She drew a vertical line on one side of the whiteboard, then turned back to the team.

'All right. Whoever this individual is, he has the means to kill someone, and dismember body parts without being disturbed. For some reason, he decides to transport those parts to another location. Then, he dumps the remains in landfill. Let's brainstorm this. What does he do for a living that means he has the tools and hiding place to commit murder and try to dispose of the bodies, and what the hell is he doing trying to burn them? Why not bury the parts where he killed them?'

She gestured to the uniformed sergeant who had raised her hand. 'Yes?'

'He might have intended to bury them, guv, but we haven't had any decent rain for over two weeks. The ground is rock solid around here at the moment.'

'Good point. Anyone else?'

'You said it when we were at the landfill site earlier,' said Barnes. 'He would have made a hell of a mess. Everyone underestimates how much blood is actually in the human body. So, he has to have somewhere he can use without being disturbed.'

'And with good drainage,' said Carys.

'Lucas's report confirmed no power tools were used,' said Gavin as he leafed through his notes, 'so our killer must be physically strong and have access to manual tools that could inflict these sorts of chop wounds.'

Kay ran her gaze over the timeline she'd written on the whiteboard. 'There's no clear pattern, either. There's nothing to indicate whether the person responsible for this has done it before or will do it again.'

She recapped the pen and tossed it onto the desk next to her in frustration. 'It's like he's gone out on a killing spree, and then stopped.'

'You think he's done this before?' said Gavin.

She pursed her lips. 'Unfortunately, yes, I do. With the exception of the foot, it's almost as if he's had practice.'

'Maybe he won't kill again,' said Debbie. 'Maybe he's done what he set out to do.'

'Either way, it doesn't help us,' said Kay. 'If he's gone to ground, we still have to find him and bring him to justice for what he's done. And, if he hasn't finished, we have to stop him before he does it again.'

She turned back to the whiteboard with a sigh and ran her hand through her hair.

'And, we still have no idea why he's doing this.'

SEVENTEEN

Kay pushed away a stack of manila folders, took one look at the growing list of emails on her computer screen, and let out a groan.

The last of the investigation team had left half an hour ago, and the incident room was silent save for an errant bluebottle that was head-butting the window above Debbie's desk in a frantic attempt to escape.

She checked her watch, surprised to discover it was nearly seven o'clock. She'd been so engrossed in her work, she hadn't heard the roar of the vacuum cleaner. The cleaners were already at the far end of the corridor outside, almost finished with their work.

She leaned forward and rested her head in her hands, closing her eyes for a moment.

Four days in to a major enquiry, and they were frustratingly short of a breakthrough of any kind.

Footsteps sounded in the corridor, followed by faint voices, and the soft *click* of the incident room door being opened reached her ears.

Kay kept her head bowed, running through the scenarios she knew off by heart, and mentally preparing new tasks for her team when they returned in the morning. It was vital to keep their momentum going; they were tight-knit and hardworking, but soon the frustration would start to show.

Having been responsible for clearing one cold case off the Division's record, she didn't intend to add another in its place.

She sensed someone approaching and opened her eyes as a steaming mug of tea was plonked down on the desk beside her.

'Thought you might want that,' said Sharp, and pulled up a chair beside her. 'What're you still doing here?'

She waved her hand at the pile of paperwork. 'I have no suspect. No murder scene. No idea who the victims are.'

He peered over his shoulder at the whiteboard at the far end of the room. 'It looks like you've taken an exhaustive approach. Sometimes these things take longer that we'd like. You'll get there.'

Kay sighed, and reached out for the tea, but Sharp shook his head.

'Hang on. You look like you could do with something stronger. Back in a minute.'

The sound of a filing cabinet drawer being opened and then slammed shut preceded him reappearing, a bottle of single malt in his hand.

Kay frowned. 'I didn't know you kept a bottle of that locked in your filing cabinet.'

'Safest place. At least Barnes can't get his hands on it.'

He grinned, took their mugs over to the kitchenette in the corner, and rinsed them out before returning and pouring a single measure of the spirit into each.

'Cheers.'

Kay clinked her mug against his, took a sip and sank back into her chair.

'Where've you been, anyway? Haven't seen you for a few days.'

'Headquarters.'

'Problem?'

'No, just politics. As usual.' He craned his neck to see the whiteboard at the far end of the room.

'Reckon your two bodies at the landfill site are linked to the foot?'

'I hope so. I'd hate to think there are two of them out there doing this.'

'Any idea who any of the remains belong to yet?'

'No. Harriet's got a forensic anthropologist on board for the landfill bodies – she reckons even with the fact the remains are burnt, they might be able to extract DNA and some other details that could help.'

Sharp turned back to her. 'I know you're frustrated but give it time. Not all cases are solved in the first few days.'

'I know that, guv, but it worries me – we've got nothing at all. Oh, a pale-coloured pickup with its licence plates missing in one photo, and stolen ones in another. That's it.'

'Can I give you some advice?'

'Please. Anything.'

Sharp drained his drink, then rose from his seat and patted her on the shoulder.

'Go home, Kay. Spend the evening with Adam. Watch a movie. Clear your head. You're not going to gain anything by sitting here letting your mind work in overdrive.'

KAY PUSHED the front door open, the aroma of a spicy curry tickling her senses as she kicked off her shoes and hurried through to the kitchen.

Adam sat at the central worktop, flicking through the local free newspaper. He raised his head as she appeared.

'Hello. I thought I heard your car pull up outside.'

She wandered around to where he sat and kissed him, before helping herself to a beer out of the refrigerator and grabbing another for him.

Placing it next to his empty glass, she frowned.

'Where's Misha? I half expected her to be running around in here, knowing what you're normally like.'

He leaned back and eyed her warily. 'She's in the dog house.'

'What has she done?'

'There's no more oregano in the garden.'

'Oh, no – I thought you and Barnes built that pen for her so she couldn't escape?'

Adam shrugged and managed to look a little guilty. 'I got home and she seemed bored cooped up in there, so I thought while I had a shower I'd let her have a run around. Won't be doing that again.'

Kay smiled. 'Ah, well. We can buy some more when she's gone.'

'I wouldn't mind, but it's a pain to grow.'

'There's nothing left of it at all?'

'No – and I hope she has a bad case of indigestion, too.'

'Is that why we're having a curry tonight instead of pasta, then?'

'Very funny. Go and get changed; I'll be dishing up in a minute.'

EIGHTEEN

The next morning, Kay had started to brief her team when the phone on Gavin's desk rang and he excused himself to take the call.

'So,' said Kay, 'Harriet confirmed late yesterday that there are remains for two victims within the area that Geoff Cornwell was working on yesterday. No other body parts have been found there. From today, they'll extend their search across the older parts of the landfill site, working with the dog unit to ascertain whether more victims have yet to be discovered.'

'Guv?'

She glanced over her shoulder from the white-board to see Gavin hovering at the edge of the group.

'What is it?'

He squeezed between two colleagues who sat at

the front of the briefing and handed her a slip of paper.

'That was a podiatrist over at Tunbridge Wells – says a patient of his missed an appointment a week ago. He thought it was unusual at the time, because the man had had recent surgery and needed to have a dressing changed. He didn't have time to phone him to chase him up last week and has only returned from a conference in Oxford this morning when he heard the news about the find at the weekend.'

A murmur of excitement filled the room as Kay ran her eyes down the message.

'Have you made an appointment to interview him?' she said.

'We're due to meet with him in an hour.'

'Good work.'

Gavin nodded, then made his way back towards Carys's desk, leaning against the wall behind her while Kay continued the briefing.

'Notwithstanding the lead Gavin's got for us, we still have other victims who we know nothing about. Debbie – anything from the missing persons database?'

The uniformed police officer rose from her seat so she could address the room.

'There are a number of missing persons in the

Kent area, some of whom have been missing for over a year or more. We've narrowed that list down to concentrate on adult males only for the time being, based on Harriet's advice on the finds yesterday. Today, I plan to work through that refined list to make sure it's up to date before we start making further enquiries with family members.'

'Good. Work with Carys to put together a summary for us by the end of today. Harriet has confirmed the forensic anthropologist is available tomorrow morning, and they'll be conducting a series of tests on the finds to see if they can extract DNA or any other information to supplement Lucas's post mortem report. Hopefully, that'll help us.'

Kay wrote an update on the whiteboard next to each action. 'Ian – have you got that list of employees from Whitman?'

Barnes held up a sheaf of paper. 'Came through this morning on email. I'm working with uniform to check through these to see if there are any prior convictions or anything like that. Whitman is also sending us CCTV footage for the past month so we can track the comings and goings for the public access to the landfill.'

'That's great, thanks.' Kay checked her watch, then recapped the pen and tossed it onto the metal shelf under the whiteboard. 'Barnes – you're in charge here while I go with Gavin to interview this podiatrist. We'll have another briefing late afternoon so we can bring you all up to date on our findings.'

KAY CHECKED her emails on her phone as Gavin shifted gear and tapped the steering wheel in frustration.

She glanced up, saw that they had only travelled another few metres towards the roundabout and the junction with the A21, and sighed.

'Jesus, this reminds me why I don't come to Tunbridge Wells as often as I used to. I swear the traffic gets worse every time.'

'This is actually quite good,' said Gavin. 'You should see it when the schools empty out at half past three.'

'Where does the podiatrist have his surgery?'

'The other side of town – over at Mount Ephraim.'

'Blimey, he must be doing all right for himself.'

Gavin smiled. 'Private practice.'

Half an hour later, he'd found a parking space on The Common close to The Mount Edgcumbe pub, and after locking the car, led the way past a large rock formation that dominated the green space to their right.

A light breeze caught Kay's hair as she followed him along the narrow road, and she took in the view across the busy town centre from the steep incline.

She could see why the town had been popular with gentrified visitors from London hundreds of years ago and still had its share of tourists year-round.

Eighteenth-century houses overlooked the Common, away from the busy town centre, interspersed with an occasional modern office between the historical buildings.

They paused at the top of the hill to negotiate the busy road, then Gavin turned right.

'It's along here,' he said, and pointed at a large house further along the street.

White stonework shone in the afternoon sunlight. Dark slates covered the roof and as Kay left the pavement and crunched across the gravel driveway that led to the front door, she found herself envying the residents who could sit in the bay windows of their homes and look out over the rest of the spa town below.

'Does he own all of this?' she said under her breath.

Gavin grinned. 'No. Most of the houses along here have been divided up into apartments, but they'll still cost you over half a million or more. Dr Andrews has the lower apartment as his practice, and he and his family live in one of the others above.'

He stepped into the porch that sheltered the front door from the elements in colder weather and pressed an intercom next to a stained-glass partition window before announcing their arrival.

A figure appeared on the other side of the door a moment later, blurred by the mottled effect of the bright colours in the glass. The door was opened and a bespectacled man in his late fifties peered out, a rueful smile on his face.

'I figured you got caught in traffic.'

'Sorry we're late, Dr Andrews,' said Gavin. He introduced Kay, and she shook hands with the specialist.

'Thanks for seeing us at short notice.'

'No problem. Please, call me Rob. Come on through to the clinic.'

As she followed the podiatrist across the tiled and spacious hallway, Kay glanced left and right at the bespoke furniture that lined the room.

To one side, a dark mahogany credenza held brochures and advertisements for local gyms and alternative therapies, while on the other a row of matching chairs sat empty.

'You're lucky, the clinic is quiet today so we don't have to rush.' Andrews opened a door to the side of the hallway and waved them through.

Kay entered a light and airy space, an enormous bay window commanding the room and providing a view across The Common while off to the far side, a stone surround fireplace was complemented by fitted bookcases to either side. A large desk was to the right of the room. Two armchairs sat on each side of the fireplace and it was to these that Andrews gestured.

'Might as well make ourselves comfortable rather than using one of the consulting rooms,' he smiled. His face grew serious as he sat at the desk and folded his hands in front of him. 'Now, I expect you'd like to get on and ask me about my missing patient.'

'If we could.' Kay waited until Gavin had rummaged in his pocket for his notebook and a pen, then turned back to Andrews. 'What can you tell us about him?'

'Clive Wallis. Forty-two years old. Single, lives in Camden Park on the other side of town.'

'What were you treating him for?'

Andrews pursed his lips. 'Issues relating to Type 2 diabetes. Unfortunately, Mr Wallis is a bit too fond of his sugary snacks and alcohol and refuses to lose weight, so he's started to experience ulcerations that are slow to heal. One particular wound got infected and I had no option but to recommend day surgery for him at the local hospital – it was more than I could deal with here.'

'And when was this?'

Andrews turned to his laptop and hit a few keystrokes, then pushed his glasses up his nose and ran a finger down the screen.

'He had surgery fourteen days ago. He was due to see me first thing Friday morning last week, so I could check how it was healing up and change the dressing to avoid infection.'

'What did you do when he missed his appointment?'

'Jenny, my receptionist, phoned his mobile number fifteen minutes after he was due, but there was no answer. I tried again later that evening and left a voicemail message for him. It was never returned, and I had to drive up to Oxford for a conference over the weekend. I had a note in my calendar to call him again today, but then I saw the headline on the Sunday newspaper my wife had put out for the recycling this morning, and that's when I phoned the police.'

'What does he do for a living?'

'Hang on. Sorry. I'll have to look it up.' Andrews' brow creased as his fingers tapped the keyboard again. 'Ah, here you go – he's an import and export consultant for a company based down at Dover. He works from home a lot of the time, but I seem to recall him saying he has to go to head office once a month for meetings and the like.'

'I don't suppose you've got a note of his employers' details?' said Kay.

'Actually, yes, I do.' Andrews reached out for a notepad and scrawled across the page before he pushed back his chair and walked around to where she sat. 'I've written down his home address, too.'

'Have you tried his home phone number?'

He shook his head. 'Doesn't have one. A lot of my patients these days have done away with landlines in favour of mobile phones.'

'And no next of kin noted on his records?'

'None at all.' He removed his glasses and stuck one of the arms in the neck of his short-sleeved shirt. 'He was an only child, apparently. Said he inherited his house from his father.'

He moved back to the desk, turning to lean against it and folded his arms. 'Look, do you think

Clive is your victim? I mean, it's a bit of a coincidence, isn't it?'

Kay rose from her chair, and Gavin followed suit.

'Too early to say at the moment.' She held out her
hand. 'Thank you very much for your time though. I
appreciate it.'

'Not at all. You know where to find me if you
need me.'

'Thanks – and if Mr Wallis should reappear,
you'll let me know?'

'Straight away, Detective Hunter.'

NINETEEN

'What now, guv?'

Kay peered over the roof of the car towards the brick buildings and slate rooftops of the centre of Tunbridge Wells, her brow creased.

'Get onto the locals. Let them know we're going to take a look at Clive Wallis's house at Camden Park and to be on standby if we need them.'

'Will do.'

Gavin ducked out of sight, his voice carrying through the open passenger door to where Kay stood, mulling over what Rob Andrews had told them.

Although she'd never admit it to the specialist, he was right – it was too much of a coincidence that his patient had gone missing without a trace, and within the timeframe Lucas's post mortem report had identified.

Yet she couldn't reconcile the thought that if the man was recovering from minor surgery, then how had he met his fate?

Surely, he would have been resting at home until his next appointment?

She blinked and tried to concentrate.

Would their killer attack Wallis at home, then risk transporting his body all the way over to Boughton Monchelsea?

And, why?

Did they know each other? Why not dump the body closer to Tunbridge Wells?

A tap on the window pulled her from her thoughts, and she glanced down as Gavin pushed the door open.

'In you get. We're on.'

'What did they say?' said Kay. She clipped her seatbelt into place while he negotiated the narrow road and squeezed their vehicle past the wing mirrors of parked cars on both sides.

'Apparently, a neighbour phoned them this morning – said she was concerned she hadn't seen Wallis for a few days and wondered if local uniform could check the hospitals to make sure he was okay. It's on the task list for today's duty roster – they hadn't got around to it yet.'

'Saves them a job, then.'

'Indeed.'

Gavin edged the car into traffic on Mount Ephraim before taking a left-hand turn that led them back towards the town centre.

Kay used the time to open a search engine app on her phone and typed in Clive Wallis's employers' details. 'This company he works for – they import wine from France and Germany, and export local wine and spirits and other foodstuff.'

'Not exactly the rough and tumble trade you'd expect to result in a murder, is it?' said Gavin. He swore under his breath as a motorcyclist swerved around their car to beat them to the mini-roundabout at the bottom of the hill.

'No, it isn't.' She checked the progress of the satellite navigation, then peered through the windscreen. 'There should be a turning on the right a bit further up here, then take the second right before the railway station.'

Moments later, Gavin reversed the car into a space opposite a semi-circle of elegant Regency homes.

Kay recalled that one of the residences had recently sold for close to one million pounds, and as she climbed from the vehicle she cast her eyes over the ornate cream brickwork and bordering beech hedgerows, and couldn't prevent the murmur of awe that escaped her lips.

'Blimey,' said Gavin as they crossed the path to the front door of the house they'd identified as Wallis's. 'What the hell did his father do for a living to be able to afford this?'

'God knows,' she said, 'but given we're within walking distance of the train station, I'll bet he worked in the City.'

'They don't even have private gardens – look; they're all communal.'

'Well, the whole park is private, so it's not like you're going to be tripping over your neighbours if you live around here.'

She broke off at the sound of another vehicle approaching and stepped out of the way as a uniform patrol car braked to a standstill beside them.

Two officers climbed out, and she introduced herself and Gavin.

'Nigel Best, ma'am,' said the shorter of the two. 'And this is Ben Allen. We were requested to attend, in case you needed a hand.'

'Thanks,' said Kay. 'Do you want to start by trying the neighbours either side? I presume it was one of them who made the report this morning.'

'Will do.'

As the two officers split up and approached the neighbouring properties, Kay turned her attention back to Wallis's house.

The curtains to the room overlooking the crescent hadn't been drawn and she negotiated a shrubbery before shielding the window with her hand and peering in.

Inside, a spacious drawing room appeared to be deserted, the furniture immaculate – even from her position she could see the gleam of polish on the mahogany legs of a chaise longue, while the room itself appeared light and airy – and devoid of its usual occupant.

She straightened at the sound of footsteps to see Best and Allen hurrying towards her.

'Both neighbours confirm he hasn't been seen since last week,' said Best. 'I checked around the back, too – the place seems deserted.'

'I don't suppose either of them had a key?'

In response, he held up a brass object.

'Good. Come on.'

They moved to the front door and she nodded to the uniformed officer who, after first knocking to ascertain whether Wallis was home, twisted the key in the lock and gave the door a shove.

It opened, and he turned to Kay when there was no response from inside to his shouted enquiry. 'With all due respect, guv, I'll check it's safe first.'

'Go on, then.'

He stepped over the threshold and disappeared off to his right, calling out Clive's name as he worked his way through the house.

Kay bit her lip and waited for what seemed an age as he moved into her line of vision before making his way upstairs.

Eventually, he returned, and shook his head. 'No-one in. You're safe to proceed, guv.'

Kay took a pair of gloves Gavin held out to her, slipped them on and moved into the hallway.

The first thing that struck her was how clean the place was – Wallis may have been a bachelor, but he was fastidious in his tidiness.

She sniffed the air.

A light scent of furniture polish teased her senses, and as she glanced over her shoulder to see Gavin making his way up the stairs, she noticed the high sheen on the black and white tiles that covered the floor.

'Yell if you need me, Gav.'

'Will do.'

'Best? Could you stay by the door and make sure none of the neighbours disturb us?'

'Guv.'

Gavin disappeared from sight, and Kay made her way through an open door and into a living area.

The walls had been painted deep green, accentuated by a selection of potted plants that had been strategically placed around the room, giving a relaxed atmosphere to the space.

A large desk took up the far end of the living area, and Kay wandered over to it, casting her gaze over the framed photographs that were displayed in one corner.

It was the first time she'd seen a picture of Wallis, and in all the photographs he was receiving awards, his face beaming with pride.

Despite the podiatrist's description of him, Kay thought the man was quite good-looking. He was tall enough that his weight seemed evenly distributed, and in all the photographs, he was immaculately dressed.

She put down the last of the frames and turned to survey the rest of the room. A bookcase stood against the wall to the left of the desk and contained a mixture of action adventure thrillers and business tomes with titles that professed to teach the reader how to influence customers and management alike.

Here was a man who appeared to live for his career.

She stopped in the middle of the room and frowned. There were no personal touches, no indication of what Wallis enjoyed outside of his working life. Not only that, there was also no computer.

She left the living room and stepped into the hallway once more. PC Best stood on the doorstep, his back to the house. Kay turned right and found a large kitchen that Adam would have drooled over. Every appliance gleamed in the sunlight that streamed through the back window, and each appliance was a top of the range choice for a discerning chef.

Except, as Kay rummaged through the cupboards and then opened the door to an empty refrigerator, it didn't appear as if Wallis ever cooked.

Her eyes fell upon a key on the worktop. She swept it up and inserted it into the lock in the back door.

Outside, she found the rubbish bin to the left of the back door and flipped the lid open.

She was rewarded with the sweet stench of

discarded pizza boxes. Batting away a fly, she closed the lid and went back to the kitchen, locking the door behind her and replacing the key.

She began to open each of the kitchen drawers, looking for anything that might give her a clue as to the man's fate, when she heard Gavin call out.

She slammed the drawer back into place, hurried across the hallway, and ran up the stairs two at a time, using the newel post at the top to slow her pace.

'What is it?'

'I think I know what's happened to Clive.'

'Where are you?'

'Bathroom. Back of the house.'

She strode along the passageway, following his voice until she found him crouched next to a vanity unit under a porcelain sink.

He rose to his feet as she appeared.

'Look. Toothbrush is missing. Half the contents of this drawer are gone – including an electric razor, and I've checked the bedroom. There are empty hangers in the wardrobe.'

Kay blinked as she processed his words. 'What about a laptop or a mobile phone?'

'No sign of any up here – you?'

'No, and no chargers for either of them downstairs.'

Kay snapped her gloves off her fingers and handed them to him before breathing a sigh of relief. 'He's not missing, is he? He's gone away.'

TWENTY

The next morning, Kay held the door to the incident room open for Sharp, then strode towards her desk and dumped her bag on it before raising her voice above the hum that filled the space.

'Everyone gather around. Front of the room, please.'

The conversations grew quiet as her colleagues joined her, a few with quizzical expressions on their faces.

She waited while chairs were dragged across the threadbare carpet and the team found places to perch on desks, then thanked them and provided an update from the previous day's activities.

'On the basis of our search at Clive Wallis's house, it appears that he may have left his home voluntarily. However, until we know for certain, Mr Wallis is to continue to be treated as a missing persons case.'

She waited while the assembled team caught up with their note-taking, then gestured to Carys. 'Can you look into his employers for me while we're here? They're based in Dover – details are on the system. Find out if they know where he is.'

'Will do, guv.' Carys moved to her desk and pulled up the relevant information on HOLMES while Kay continued.

'What's the progress on the CCTV from the land-fill site? Anyone?'

A uniformed officer next to Carys's desk stepped forward. 'We've obtained the footage from three of the four cameras at the site,' he said. 'Two of those are no use to us – they show the vehicle compound where the excavators and everything are kept, as well as the site office. We'll start to go through the others for the gate and the public right of way today.'

Kay frowned. 'It would've made more sense to do those first.'

'Yes, guv – the problem was, none of the files were named properly, so it was a bit hit and miss until we realised what they'd done.'

'All right. As fast as you can, though.'

The phone on Kay's desk trilled, and Barnes stuck his hand up. 'I'll get it.'

'Thanks.' Kay turned back to the whiteboard. 'What about statements from the other employees at the landfill site?'

Debbie cleared her throat. 'We've completed those and they're all in the system now. No-one has reported any unusual activity, and there are no other cases of suspicious items being found on site.'

'What about past convictions for any employees?'

'Only one bloke – Justin Tinner. Two months for possession of drugs when he was nineteen. Been clean since, and that's going on six years.'

Kay noticed Carys ending her phone call and waited as she made her way back to the group. 'Anything useful?'

'I spoke with Clive Wallis's HR manager. She says she last saw him at a conference at a hotel outside Maidstone last week. She said he was hobbling a bit, but fine. Hasn't been seen since – they're about to write to him and issue a formal warning.'

Kay caught Gavin's brow furrow, noting she probably wore the same perplexed expression.

'When did the conference finish?'

'Thursday, apparently.'

'And yet all his personal effects are still missing from his house.'

'Guv?' Barnes was holding up his hand to get her attention. He replaced the desk phone back in its cradle, then moved back to where the group gathered and elbowed his way past a couple of junior members of the uniformed team, holding out a piece of paper to her as he drew closer. 'That was Lucas – he confirms we've got a match between the amputated foot and some of the other body parts found at the landfill.'

Kay scanned the page, then raised her gaze to Carys. 'You might want to suggest to Wallis's employers that they hold fire with that plan to issue a formal warning to him until we speak with them.'

Carys's eyebrows shot upwards. 'You think it's him?'

Kay exhaled. 'Could be. Lucas needs a DNA sample to confirm it. Can you get onto Tunbridge Wells and ask them to take a swab from the house? Gavin – with me. Let's go and find out what Wallis's employers can tell us.'

TWENTY-ONE

Kay and Gavin set off for Dover as soon as the briefing concluded, and although the morning rush hour traffic had passed, it took Gavin over an hour to reach the busy port town.

They passed a steady stream of articulated trucks on the M20, many of them with intercontinental licence plates and colourful logos adorning the trailers. The opposite carriageway was as busy, with goods from the ferry terminal being transported across the south of England towards their destinations.

When they entered the town via the main road, Gavin's mouth turned down as he surveyed graffiti tags that adorned the boarded-up shop windows.

'Some things don't change. I was a probationary

constable here for six months,' he said. 'That was an eye-opener.'

'They usually pick an interesting one for your first year.'

'What about you? Where did you do your training?'

'Tonbridge. Loved it.'

'Lucky you. Did you always want to be a detective?'

'Yes. I applied as soon as I could and volunteered for any opportunity to help with a major investigation that came along – same as Debbie does. There were a couple of years where Adam and I hardly saw each other – we really were like passing ships. There was me trying to work my way up the career ladder with Kent Police, and him eager to set up his own veterinary practice.'

'How did he manage it in the end?'

Kay dropped her mobile phone into her bag. 'He'd been caring for a couple of horses for an old woman who lived on a smallholding near Tenterden. She rescued them from being sent to an abattoir after their racing careers were over, and he used to go over there once a month to check them over. Wouldn't take any money off her for it – you know what he's like. He spent a lot of time chatting with her, too while he was there and often did odd jobs around the place at weekends if I was working. I think she was lonely; her husband had died years before and they'd had no children, and she enjoyed Adam's company. When she died, we got a hell of a shock – it turned out she was very well off and left him the house on Weavering Street and the smallholding on the condition he continued to care for the horses.'

'Wow.'

'I know. He had no idea. She'd never said anything to him, but I think she wanted to make sure those horses were in good hands after she died, and he was the only person she trusted. We lived at the smallholding at Tenterden for a couple of years until the horses died, and then sold that and moved back to Maidstone.'

'And he used the money from the smallholding sale to start up the clinic?'

'Yes – hasn't looked back since. Loves his work, as you know, and now the clinic is established he can afford to bring on younger veterinarians to train them.'

Gavin flicked the indicator to turn left and gestured through the windscreen at an imposing three-storey building that towered over the low-set industrial units around it.

'This is the place.'

Smoked glass obscured Kay's view of the inside of the building, but when they pushed through the single door, she was surprised to find herself in a large light and airy space that belied the outer façade.

The woman behind the reception desk waved them to a group of chairs around a low table at the far end of the atrium.

The chairs were built to impress, rather than for comfort, and Kay resisted the urge to fidget while she waited.

Thankfully, Clive Wallis's employer didn't keep them long, and she turned to see an enormous man bearing down on them.

His appearance gave her the impression he imbibed his own food and wine imports on a regular basis. His mouth formed a broad smile as he approached.

'Montgomery Fisher, general manager for sales,' he barked, and thrust out his hand. 'Call me Monty.'

Kay managed not to wince as he crushed her hand within his and breathed a sigh of relief as he let go and turned to the receptionist.

'Got a room free, Sharon?'

'Conference room,' said the woman. 'I put a pot of coffee on.'

'Good lass.' He turned back to Kay and Gavin. 'Come on through.'

For such a large man, he moved with ill-concealed haste, as if every precious minute with them prevented him from another sale – or meal.

He swung a door open and stepped to one side to let them pass, then gestured to the eight seats placed around a highly polished conference table.

'Coffee?'

'Please,' said Kay.

She positioned herself in the nearest chair facing the door, Gavin taking the one next to her and they waited while Fisher fussed over the coffee machine.

He slid a cup and saucer towards Gavin, placed Kay's in front of her and eased himself into a seat opposite them before tearing two sugar sachets open and stirring them into his drink.

'Right, so your colleague said on the phone you wanted to talk to me about Clive Wallis. What do you want to know? I take it Hayley in HR told her we were about to issue him with a formal warning?'

'Yes, can I ask why that is?' said Kay.

'He's been absent since Thursday's sales confer-ence, that's why. Our permanent staff are expected to phone us immediately if they're unable to work, and we haven't heard from him for over a week now. It's unacceptable.'

'Is it out of character?'

'Yes, but you have to understand – we've had to make a number of redundancies earlier this year; business hasn't been doing as well as it ought, and Clive was one of the ones we agreed to keep on board. Last week's get-together was set up in order to gee everyone up a bit, get them refocused after the rough patch we all went through. Cost a fortune, mind. And then Clive hasn't been seen since.'

'This "get-together" as you call it. Where was that held? Here?'

'God, no.' He spread his hands expansively. 'This is the biggest room we've got. No good at all. A lot of our permanent sales staff work from home, like Clive. Helps to keep the overheads down, you see? Meant we didn't have to take a lease out on bigger premises, thank goodness.'

'So, where was it held?' said Gavin, turning the page of his notebook.

'That new hotel on the A20 outside Maidstone. Can't remember the name of it. Sharon sorted it out. Two days of executive training – team building, that sort of thing, then everyone got given their sales targets for the rest of the year. Bloody expensive, like I said. But, it gets them all together in one place – they work autonomously, so it's good for morale, especially at the moment.'

'What day did the conference finish?'

'Thursday. Everyone got there Wednesday from about lunchtime onwards. There were some activities and things held in the afternoon to break the ice – golf, team building games, that sort of thing. Then, we had the sales training on the Thursday morning. They were all on their way home by four o'clock that afternoon.'

'And you haven't heard from Mr Wallis since?'

'No.' Fisher leaned back in his seat and folded his arms. 'Hate to think he's gone off and met with a competitor. Some of the information shared in the conference on Thursday morning was bloody confidential.'

'And you've been trying to contact him?'

'Daily. Phone and email. Like I said to your colleague, our next step is to issue him with a formal notice. We can't have our staff going off like this. It's unacceptable.'

'Did you know he had been in hospital the previous week?'

He frowned. 'Only a minor procedure on his foot,

as I understand. He was hobbling a bit but didn't seem to be in too much discomfort.'

'Why would he attend the conference if he'd been in hospital?' said Kay.

Fisher sighed and fiddled with his tie. 'Look, like I said, times are tough. He may have thought that if he didn't turn up, then he'd be next in line for the chop.'

'Did you threaten him?'

'Of course not.' A faint blush began at his neck and worked its way north. 'That's not legal, for a start.'

'Do you have a next of kin on Mr Wallis's personnel file? Anyone who might be able to help us understand where he might be?' said Kay.

'I'll have to ask Hayley. If there are, she would've tried to contact them as well.'

Kay smiled. 'Thanks. We'll wait.'

She turned to Gavin as the sales manager left the room, and he held up his mobile.

'Text message from Barnes. Tunbridge Wells got the swab and it was couriered to Lucas immediately. I've asked him to text me the minute he hears back from the pathology lab.'

Kay nodded, then sat back in her chair as Fisher returned, a slim file in his hand.

He hesitated a moment, then slid it across the table to her.

'You understand that I can't let you walk out of here with that unless I have a formal request?'

'That's fine.'

She flicked open the file and scanned the meagre contents until she found what she was looking for. The section of Clive's employee details where a next of kin would normally be noted was blank.

'No family?'

'His father died some years ago from complications arising from diabetes and his mother passed away a year or so ago,' said Fisher. 'Left him the house. A bit sad, really. I don't think he has much of a social life. Never seems to talk about it, anyway.'

She shoved the file back towards Fisher as a two-tone *beep* reached her ears.

'Guv.'

She took the phone Gavin held out to her, scanned the message, then rose from her seat before handing it back and turning to the sales manager.

'Last question, Mr Fisher. What's the name of the hotel you used for the conference?'

TWENTY-TWO

'Lucas? Just got your message. What can you tell me?'

Kay shoved the phone into the hands-free cradle on the dashboard and turned on the speakerphone mode so Gavin could hear both sides of the conversation as he drove back towards Maidstone, the speedometer hovering a little over the national speed limit.

'Okay, so we've got Clive Wallis's blood test results from his GP together with the samples we took from the amputated foot. We've also extracted DNA from the foot, the bones found at the landfill and ran a comparison with the DNA swab taken from a water glass in his bathroom by your colleagues at Tunbridge

Wells. You're lucky it's a quiet week at the laboratory – you'd normally have to wait at least a week.'

'I know, thank you. So, it's definitely a match with Wallis?'

'We're certain.'

Kay exhaled, some of the tension leaving her shoulders. 'That's great work, Lucas. Thank you. Please thank Harriet and her team for me as well – I realise that was hard work at the landfill site for them.'

'No problem.'

'What about the second victim?'

'Nothing at the moment – those results have yet to come back. I'll be in touch with my formal report as soon as possible.'

Kay ended the call and glanced up as the vehicle shot underneath a gantry. A blue and white sign displayed the distance to the county town, and she tried not to let her impatience show as the traffic crawled to a standstill outside Ashford.

'What next, guv?'

Gavin's voice jerked her from her thoughts.

'Straight to the hotel that Wallis stayed at.'

She scrolled through the contacts on Gavin's phone until she found the name she was seeking, then hit the dial button.

Barnes answered within three rings.

'Gav?'

'It's me,' said Kay. 'We're on speakerphone. We've heard from Lucas – you'll get a copy of an email he's sending to me shortly, but he's confirmed he's got a match on one of our victims as being Wallis.'

'How did you get on in Dover?'

'There's no next of kin, but his manager, Montgomery Fisher, confirmed he was last seen at a sales conference and team building exercise held over two days last week at that new hotel just off the M20 at Maidstone. We're heading there now. Can you organise the paperwork to get us access to their personnel files? I'm going to try and have a look at the hotel's security video footage when we get there.'

'Will do. What was Wallis doing there the day after leaving hospital?'

'Trying to keep his job, by the sounds of it.'

She ended the call as the traffic started to move forwards once more, and within fifteen minutes Gavin had found the hotel and parked in a space close to its reception doors.

As Kay climbed from the car, she noticed a group of four men in light coloured trousers and pastel short-sleeved shirts making their way from the car park to an opening in a hedgerow on the far right of the hotel. A sign next to the ornamental planting proclaimed the newest eighteen-hole golf course in Kent and promises of weekly competitions for enthusiastic locals.

'Wonder how they stay in business?' said Kay. 'There's another hotel a few miles from here with a golf course, isn't there? Makes you wonder how this lot are doing, having to compete with an established hotel.'

'Lots of businesses in the county need a central conferencing location, guv and golf's a popular game.'

She wrinkled her nose, and Gavin chuckled as she joined him on the steps leading up to the reception area before holding the door open for her.

The receptionist, a man in his twenties with far too much enthusiasm for a Friday afternoon as far as Kay was concerned, leapt to his feet as they approached, a wide smile creasing his mouth.

'Can I help you?'

His cheery demeanour faltered when Kay flipped open her warrant card.

'I need to speak to the duty manager,' she said.

'I'm afraid he's with a group of delegates from one of our shareholding companies at the moment.'

'That's fine. Please let him know we're here to discuss the possible murder of one of your hotel guests and we'll be waiting here for him. No doubt the local media will be wanting to speak to him at some point, too, but with any luck the timing of our visit will help him ward them off and save this hotel – and its shareholders – from any embarrassment that may cause.'

The receptionist let out a shocked gasp, his face turning white, before he reached out and punched a series of numbers into his desk phone.

Kay turned from the desk and led Gavin towards four armchairs surrounding a low coffee table and picked up one of the hotel's brochures as she sat.

The receptionist's voice reached her, a flustered tone accentuated by his shock.

Gavin grinned. 'That was mean.'

'I know, but we don't have time to mess around, Gav. We're almost a week into this investigation and we have no leads. Time to up the ante.'

Five minutes later, the sound of hurrying footsteps reached her ears and she glanced up from the brochure as a thin man with black hair advanced on her, his brow furrowed.

'Detective Inspector Hunter?'

She rose from her chair and shook his outstretched hand before introducing Gavin.

'I'm Kevin Tavistock, senior duty manager. Come this way. My office is through here.'

Kay rolled the brochure between her fingers and followed Tavistock through an opening next to the reception desk into an office at the back of the hotel.

A roster had been scrawled across a whiteboard fastened to the wall at the far end, with a note of the more important guests who were expected over the weekend.

Tavistock waved them to two grey plastic seats that faced a desk in the corner and eased himself into a chair behind it, wiggling a mouse to awaken the computer before him.

'I understand you wanted to speak to me about one of our guests?'

The words escaped his lips in a single breath, and Kay wondered whether it was through shock or excitement.

She suspected the latter.

She recited the formal caution before continuing. 'I have to insist that what we discuss here is treated with the utmost confidentiality.'

'Of course, of course.' Tavistock leaned his elbows on the desk. 'What do you need to know?'

'First of all, can you confirm that Clive Wallis was a guest of your hotel last week?' said Gavin, and flipped open his notebook.

Tavistock turned to his computer and hit a few keystrokes, then nodded. 'Yes. Here he is. Part of a delegation that was booked into one of our conference rooms on Thursday. We keep a note of all names for any dietary requirements, plus of course security in the event of a fire or something like that.'

Kay raised the brochure. 'I understand from Mr Wallis's employers that part of their conference included team building exercises organised by the hotel. Can you tell me which ones?'

'Of course. Let me see... they arrived here on Wednesday afternoon and after a light lunch, they attended the craft workshop. That's where we offer guests the chance to try their hand at traditional local crafts, such as basket weaving and things. For the team building, I believe there was some sort of competition involved.' He smiled benevolently as he scanned the screen for the details. 'A few of our corporate clients are firm believers in getting their staff to work together more closely through practical exercises. Oh, here we go – archery. Got quite rowdy, according to a couple of our older guests.'

When neither Kay nor Gavin responded, he

cleared his throat. 'Erm, after that they played a few holes of golf, then we organised a barbecue for them on the terrace. The next day, their sales conference was held in the Majestic Room on the first floor. Morning tea at ten-thirty, lunch on the terrace at one o'clock, and farewell drinks at four.'

'And which room did he stay in?' said Gavin.

More keystrokes followed, then silence.

Tavistock frowned. 'I'm sorry. I have no record of Mr Wallis staying with us on either the Wednesday or the Thursday night. It only says here that he attended the conference.'

'We'll need a list of the delegates to compare with what we have from his employers, and we'd also like to interview the members of staff on duty that day,' said Kay.

The man's top lip curled. 'Well, I'll obviously need the necessary authorisations.'

'We'll have them to you before close of business today.'

'It'll be difficult to get all the staff together, too – they work different shift patterns and the duty roster was only changed yesterday morning.'

Kay rose from her seat and forced a smile as she held out her hand. 'I have a team of officers assisting with this investigation who are more than capable of coordinating interviews. We'll be in touch.'

The man managed a faint smile as they left the office, and Kay led the way back through reception to the car park beyond.

Once outside, Gavin turned to her and shoved his hands in his pockets as he stared up at the hotel's logo emblazoned across the porch above their heads.

'All right. If he didn't stay here, where the hell was he on Wednesday and Thursday night?'

TWENTY-THREE

'Settle down, you lot.'

Kay paced the floor in front of the whiteboard, conscious of Sharp hovering at the sidelines.

As soon as she'd returned to the police station, she'd knocked on his office door and spent the next half an hour arguing the case for more resources to help with her investigation.

Sharp hadn't been the problem, but headquarters was reluctant to spend the money and it had taken all of her patience and Sharp's diplomatic skills to coerce the additional funding for overtime.

Finally, they'd acquiesced, and now she was faced with the task of informing her team their weekend plans had changed.

The last uniformed officer had collapsed into a

spare chair at the front of the group with an apologetic smile. Kay held out a sheaf of paper to Barnes who stood at the right-hand side of the arc of team members.

'Take one and pass them along,' she said. 'I'm sorry, but today's events have left me with no choice but to insist on us continuing our investigation over the weekend.'

No sound emitted from the group, for which she was grateful. Her team were professionals and would do all they could to catch the killer in their midst.

'We're going to spend the next two days interviewing the staff at the hotel where Clive Wallis was last seen. According to both his employer and the hotel manager, Wallis turned up on the Wednesday to participate in a team building and sales conference event that lasted until Thursday afternoon. We have a problem.' Kay turned and tapped Wallis's photograph. 'According to the hotel's booking system, he didn't stay overnight at the hotel as planned. So, where did he go?'

She faced the group once more. 'On the sheet of paper in front of you, you'll find a note of who you've been teamed up with and a list of the people you're tasked with interviewing. We'll concentrate on hotel staff tomorrow, then the people who run the extracurricular activities on the Sunday. A lot of the businesses that provide the activities are managed by local craftsman and the like, so you may need to interview them at home if they're not at work. Debbie's very kindly collated all the relevant email addresses and phone numbers you need to give you a head start.'

She paused and took a sip of water before placing the plastic cup on the desk next to her. 'Update the database as you work, and flag anything suspicious with myself, Barnes, Gavin or Carys immediately. Any questions?'

A flurry of hands went up, and Kay spent the next twenty minutes fielding queries and fine-tuning some of the tasks until she was satisfied the team had everything they needed.

'Right, the hotel manager has allocated one of the smaller conference rooms to us for our use tomorrow, but it won't be locked, so under no circumstances leave any information regarding this investigation laying around, is that understood?'

'Guv.'

'Guv.'

'I'm sure our friends in the media will cotton on to us conducting these enquiries tomorrow, so if you experience any trouble, let me or DCI Sharp know.'

Kay glanced at the clock on the wall, then back to her team and forced a smile. 'You're all doing a great job, so thank you. We'll reconvene here as a group on Monday morning. I'll be at the hotel helping to conduct the interviews as well, so if you need me in the meantime, come and get me. Dismissed.'

Sharp wandered across to her as the team dispersed, and she turned to him with a sigh.

'Well, at least everyone was polite enough not to grumble about the weekend to my face.'

'They know you'd only ask if you had no other choice. Don't worry about it. They want to catch this killer as much as you do.'

Her gaze fell upon the photographs on the white-board. 'What if we can't, Devon? What if he's done what he's set out to do? What if he's disappeared?'

He reached out and patted her arm. 'Then we'll find him, Kay. That's what we do, remember?'

'Yeah.'

He jerked his thumb over his shoulder at her colleagues as they shut down their computers for the night and began to leave the room. 'Go on. Get home. You've got a busy day ahead of you tomorrow, and you're going to need a decent night's rest. It'll be bedlam at the hotel in the morning, mark my words.'

Kay's mobile phone began to ring, and she smiled at the familiar number on the screen.

'Hi, Abby,' she said.

'Hang on.' A muffled voice scolded someone in the background before returning. 'Sorry about that – kids are being a handful at the moment. I was checking you were still okay to catch up for my birthday next month?'

Kay smiled. Her sister had managed to persuade their parents to babysit the children for a weekend so Abby and her husband could have a relaxing weekend to celebrate her birthday, with Kay and Adam due to join them at a country retreat in Surrey.

'That's the plan. I'm even going to wear that red dress I bought months ago.'

'Bloody hell.'

They laughed, and then the phone on Kay's desk lit up and she groaned.

'Can I get back to you? I've got to take this one.'

She ended the call and picked up the other phone while stuffing her mobile into her handbag.

'Hello?'

'It's Jonathan Aspley. Got an update for me?'

'No, I haven't.'

'What were you doing at the Belvedere Hotel?'

Kay dropped her bag on the desk, stunned. 'Are you following me?'

'You didn't answer the question.'

'I'm not going to. Back off, Jonathan. You're walking on thin ice.'

'Is there a connection between the victim and the hotel?'

'We're conducting a number of enquiries in relation to our investigation.'

'Don't stonewall me, Hunter.'

'Goodbye.'

Kay slammed the phone back into its cradle and glared at it, then swiped her car keys and bag off the desk and stormed from the room.

TWENTY-FOUR

Kay parked her car in the far corner of the hotel car park the following morning, the spaces nearer the reception doors signposted with warnings that read "guests only" providing a clear indication of the hotel manager's feelings about her investigative team descending upon the business at a weekend.

She shouldered her bag, aimed her key fob at the car door to lock it, then strode across the asphalt, her jaw set.

As she pushed through the reception doors and made her way across to the desk, she noted the subtle notes of piped music filtering through the space, no doubt an effort by the same manager to add a nuance of calm to offset the number of uniformed officers milling about.

Moments later, Kevin Tavistock appeared, his face flustered as he jabbed a clipboard in her direction.

'Detective Hunter, I must insist that your people move away from the reception area immediately. Goodness knows what our guests will think.'

Kay forced a smile. 'Not a problem. Can you show me the rooms that have been allocated to us, and we'll make a start?'

He huffed, then spun on his heel and called over his shoulder. 'Through here.'

She noticed Barnes and Carys hovering next to a fire exit on the far side of the reception area.

'Come with me – Tavistock is showing me where we can set up. Where's Gavin?'

'On his way,' said Carys. 'About five minutes out. He said he was going to stop by the incident room and pick up extra stationery in case we need it.'

They fell into step beside her, the duty manager leading them through a catacomb of corridors until he stopped at a dead end.

He gestured to a set of industrial-sized kettles, water jugs brimming with ice cubes and a stack of glassware and teacups that had been organised across two tables.

'My staff will ensure these are refilled on a

regular basis,' he said. He moved to a closed door next to one of the tables and handed Kay a key. 'You and I are the only ones who have a key to this room. Come on through.'

He unlocked the door and led the way into a large conference space with tables and chairs set out in rows. Power extension leads snaked across the patterned carpet, and a whiteboard and overhead projector had been left on a table at the far side of the room.

Light poured through the windows that lined the wall to Kay's left, and she blinked to adjust her sight after the dim and dowdy hotel corridor.

'Will this be sufficient?'

She turned to the duty manager. 'It's perfect, thank you. What about rooms for interviews?'

'You'll find two more doors off the main corridor opposite the refreshment tables. They can't be locked, but they do have tables and chairs and power sockets for your equipment.'

'That doesn't matter; we won't be leaving anything behind when we finish this afternoon.'

Tavistock clasped his hands together. 'All right, well if you've got everything you need?'

'Yes, thank you.'

He nodded, then hurried from the room.

Kay turned on her heel, mentally preparing for the onslaught of a busy enquiry team descending upon the peace and quiet, then turned to Barnes and Carys.

'Okay, you two – round up everyone and we'll get started, shall we?'

———

KAY WATCHED the uniformed officers file from the room, the briefing concluded.

Each one carried a list of hotel employees and contractors who would be interviewed over the next few hours, their responses entered into the HOLMES database by Debbie West and two of her colleagues who sat closest to the whiteboard with their laptops open.

Kay hoped that by filtering the information as it was received from the interviews, the team would have a head start on processing it all when they returned to the incident room at Maidstone police station on Monday morning.

'Guv? Me and Carys are going to head over and start interviewing the activities teachers,' said Gavin, hooking his jacket on the back of a spare chair and rolling up his sleeves.

'Sounds good. I'll be here if you need me –

Barnes has gone to speak with the groundsmen. Who are you starting with?'

Carys checked her notes. "Marjory Phillips – runs a local horse riding school and offers pony trekking for guests. That wasn't offered to Clive Wallis and his colleagues according to their itinerary, but the horse riding trail borders the back of the hotel grounds, so we thought we'd better speak to her.'

'Good plan,' said Kay.

'Thanks, and after that we've got the woman who runs the orienteering classes,' said Gavin.

Carys flipped the page on her clipboard. 'Finally, Kyle Craig. Runs the archery lessons. That should take us up to lunchtime, and then we'll check back here to find out who's left.'

'Perfect, thanks.'

Kay watched them hurry from the room, then leaned against one of the desks and tried to relax.

TWENTY-FIVE

Gavin eased the pool vehicle into the hotel car park, exhaling as he applied the handbrake. He ran a hand over his face as he tore the keys from the ignition.

'Good grief, could that woman be even more exhausting to deal with?'

Carys laughed and let her seatbelt roll back into its housing before she opened her door. 'Well, I suppose if she teaches orienteering for this place, she's got to have lots of energy. Those groups can cover a serious amount of mileage.'

'I know, but on top of the other one that runs the stables, I'm worn out from listening to them.'

'And here was me thinking you were a super-fit surfer.' Carys tutted under her breath. 'Had me fooled.'

Gavin rolled his eyes and climbed out the car, waving the key fob over his shoulder to lock it and hurrying to catch up with his colleague.

'It's the amount of talking that I found exhausting. If that was two blokes, we'd have been in and out within half an hour each, tops.'

Carys narrowed her eyes at him. 'Yeah, but we probably would have had to go back and ask for more information. At least this way, we've got two thorough interviews under our belts. Useful, too.'

'Bet the one with the archery teacher goes faster.'

A coachload of tourists cluttered the asphalt apron in front of the building, the vehicle's engine ticking as it cooled. Foreign voices filled the air as each person tried to locate their suitcase while an exasperated driver attempted to steer them towards the reception area.

Carys slowed as they approached the doors and frowned as she read the signs on the side of the building, each pointing in a different direction. 'Which way is the archery course, anyway?'

'It's round the back, over to the left. Come on, it'll be quicker to go around the outside than fight our way through this lot.'

She fell into step beside him, and Gavin held back

a tendril of unruly wisteria as they moved along a narrow pathway beside the hotel.

'Thanks. Have you heard anything about the new DS?'

'No, you?'

'Nothing. Not since Kay and Sharp interviewed those candidates last week. I got the impression it didn't go too well.'

'Oh?'

'Two were from other areas, and one had a crush on Kay.'

Gavin laughed. 'Bet that went down well.'

'Yeah. It'll be weird with someone else coming on board, though won't it?'

'After all we've been through, you mean? Yeah, it will.' He paused as they reached the edge of a large turfed area at the end of the path and turned to face her. 'You weren't tempted to apply?'

Carys's brow creased. 'I was, but I had a long hard think about it, and I don't reckon I've got enough experience under my belt yet. If I apply for something like that, I want to know I'm in with a good chance, do you know what I mean?'

He nodded. 'Makes sense. Full credit to you for making that decision. I know how much you want to make this job a long-term career. I don't know if I'd want the extra responsibility to be honest.'

'Ah, see what you think when you've been a DC for another couple of years. You might change your mind.'

'Maybe.' He squinted in the bright sunlight, then pointed across to where a low barn-like structure rose above the turf at the far end. 'That must be the archery centre.'

Carys glanced to each side of where they stood. 'Think it's safe to walk across?'

'There are no targets out. Tell you what, you go in front and if I see any arrows flying, I'll tell you to duck.'

'Very funny.'

As they drew closer, Gavin spotted a figure moving within the gloom of the building's main door, his face in shadow while he worked.

The man straightened when they approached, his dark eyes taking in the two detectives before he pushed a mop of corn-coloured hair from his eyes and nodded.

'You'll be the police, then?'

Gavin made the introductions. 'I can see you're busy, Mr Craig, so we won't take up too much of your time. Just some routine questions about one of the guests that was staying here a week ago.'

Craig shifted his weight, then turned and hung the bows he'd been holding on a rack to the right of the door. 'No problem. What did you want to know?'

Carys held out a photograph of Clive Wallis. 'Do you recognise him?'

Craig peered at the picture but didn't take it from her. 'Yeah, I do. Him and a bunch of others spent an hour here during the middle of the week. Wednesday, from memory although I'd have to check the bookings. Some sort of team building thing going on.' He took a step back and frowned. 'What's he done?'

'He's dead,' said Gavin.

'Bloody hell. I mean, sorry. When?'

'That's what we're trying to ascertain,' said Carys. 'Did you spend much time with him?'

Craig rubbed his chin with a grubby hand. 'Only as much as the others. A couple of them had tried archery before, so I could spend more time with the rest of the group getting them up to speed. Probably only spoke to him individually a couple of times.'

'What did you think of him? Did he seem concerned by anything?' said Gavin.

'No – not really.' He jerked a thumb over his shoulder. 'We keep a refrigerator here for drinks and the like. Licensed, of course being on the hotel premises. Your chap didn't seem that interested in the activities. Seemed content to drink beer and chat with his colleagues. Mind you, it's a shame – he looked like he could do with a bit of exercise. Big bloke. Didn't look too healthy, although the women in the group seemed to like him enough.'

'Oh?'

He smiled. 'I think he fancied himself as a bit of a ladies' man. Certainly had them enthralled. It was all I could do to get them to shoot some arrows.'

'Any problems with anyone else in the group?'

'None that I recall. Quite an easy bunch to work with to be honest. Wish they were all like that.'

Gavin turned and took in the grounds to either side of the shed. 'This all looks new. How long have you been here?'

'About two weeks. We used to have our shed over there – further into the woodland. There's a glade through there, really nice.' He shrugged. 'Anyway, the hotel's doing so well, they've decided to expand it – you see all that construction work? They're clearing the ground between the far end of the existing building up to where the woodland finishes here, and then they'll extend it. I heard they were putting in a heated pool and spa, as well as a wedding venue.'

'How long have you worked here, Mr Craig?'

'About two and a half years. They'd just opened when I got the interview and were keen to offer different activities for guests, and I'd done this before over near Gloucestershire. As soon as they had the outbuildings and everything ready to go, I started.'

'All right,' said Gavin. 'I think that's everything for now. Thanks for your time.'

The archery teacher raised his hand in farewell and returned to his work, and Gavin led the way back towards the hotel.

'Hungry yet?' said Carys.

'Starving. But, let's have a look at that construction site first.'

TWENTY-SIX

Kay rose from her seat, stretched her arms above her head and stifled a yawn before calling over her shoulder to Debbie.

'Will you be okay here for a bit? I'm going to grab something to eat and get some fresh air.'

'No problem.'

'I'll make sure the caterers bring in something to keep you going – the way some of those constables were eyeing up the spread out there, you'd think they hadn't eaten for a month.'

'I wondered that myself. Just don't put any of that cake on my plate, okay? I'm trying to be good – I've only got a month until my holiday.'

Kay pushed open the door into the corridor and assessed the spread of food that had been arranged on a second table next to the soft drinks and hot water urns.

She'd agreed with Sharp that they'd spend some of their allocated budget on catering for the investigative team at the hotel rather than send them away to get their own food.

It helped to keep the focus on getting through the interviews over the course of the day, and the team would be less inclined to take a longer break than necessary.

She saw one of the hotel staff approaching and, after ensuring Debbie would be well looked after, she grabbed a plate for herself and piled it with a selection of sandwiches and pieces of fruit.

'Budge up, some of us are starving.'

She glanced over her shoulder at the sound of Barnes's voice, and smiled. 'How has your morning been going?'

'Not bad.' He lowered his voice as he reached out for one of the cake slices. 'Want to sit outside? Less chance of being overheard.'

He jerked his head towards the staff member who was still hovering, and she nodded.

'Lead the way.'

At the end of the corridor, Barnes pushed open a fire exit door to his right and held it open for her.

She stepped into a shaded courtyard garden at the back of the hotel that gave them an uninterrupted view of the golf course.

Shrubs and ferns filled the flower borders against the plain brickwork of the building, and newly-planted saplings swayed in the breeze and provided a little shade over a group of tables and chairs that clustered together in one corner.

'Perfect.'

'Yeah – I thought so, too. Spotted it while we were talking to one of the groundsmen.'

He pulled out a metal chair for her next to a round table, and they began to devour their food.

'God, this is great,' said Kay. 'I hate to think how much they're going to charge Sharp for this.'

'Best we make the most of it then. Could be the last time he does it.'

'True.'

'What do you make of this case then, guv?' he said, wiping his fingers with a paper napkin.

She sighed. 'Sharp keeps reminding me that it's early days and that I shouldn't get frustrated, but I can't help feeling it's going to be a long slog. The press are going to have an absolute field day if we don't solve this one quickly, Ian.'

'Don't panic yet – we've only recently found out

who our first victim is. Once Harriet and Lucas can identify the second victim, we'll be in a better position to see if there's a link between the two.'

Kay dabbed her lips then scrunched up her napkin onto her plate and sighed. 'What a horrible way to go. And Clive Wallis – he had no-one who cared about him. It all seems rather sad, doesn't it?'

Barnes landed a gentle punch on her arm. 'That's why he's got us. We'll fight his corner for him, right?'

She managed a smile, squinting in the bright sunshine. 'Right.'

Barnes followed her line of sight and shielded his eyes. 'Blimey, those two are keen. Have they had a break yet?'

Kay watched as Carys and Gavin walked around the corner at the opposite end of the hotel and headed towards a pile of rubble at the back of the building where three workmen were using shovels and pick-axes to break up an old pathway that led to a wooded area.

'I don't think so,' she said. 'They must've got back from the stables ages ago.'

'Orienteering after that, and then archery wasn't it?'

'Yeah. How did you get on this morning?'

'The chap who runs the golf centre was a bit

useless, but I fared better with one of the groundsmen – Peter Radcliffe. He definitely recalls seeing Wallis on the Wednesday afternoon. Apparently, they only played nine holes because it was so hot and they arrived too late to do the full course. He says Wallis played fairly well, seemed to get on all right with his colleagues, and that he even remembered to thank him for the hire of the clubs afterwards.' Barnes grinned. 'Apparently, not all the guests are as polite.'

'Did he mention whether he saw Wallis in the evening?'

'No – I asked him, but he only works until six o'clock. He was running late clearing up after the last of the delegates had left the course, and he went straight home afterwards.'

Kay reached over for the glass of orange juice she'd brought outside with her and took a sip. 'I'm beginning to think we're clutching at straws.'

'Yeah, but you know what it's like. We might hear something that will help.' Barnes spread his hands expansively. 'I mean, look at this place. If Wallis didn't go to his room, he could've been anywhere.'

Kay shrugged, conceding the point.

'Okay, but where did he go?'

TWENTY-SEVEN

Trudy Evans shuffled in the seat opposite Kay and twitched the hem of her skirt.

'I've never been interviewed by the police before,' she said, and gave a nervous laugh.

Kay ignored the comment as she leaned against the desk and waited while Barnes turned to a fresh page in his notebook.

She admired her colleague's interviewing skills – Barnes was a formidable investigator. The pacing of his interviews made him appear calm and collected, even if Kay knew that under the façade the man was as eager as she was to get through the list of names and begin to extrapolate the information that might lead them to their killer.

Rushing wasn't an option.

'Mrs Evans, how long have you been an employee at the hotel?' said Barnes.

'Oh, about three years. Ever since I moved here from Bristol. I'm only meant to be part-time, but there's always something to do.'

Kay said nothing when the woman smiled at her. It wasn't her interview, and she didn't want to shift the balance in the conversation.

Eventually the woman turned back to Barnes, her smile fading.

'What time did your shift start on the Wednesday?' he said.

'About ten o'clock,' said Trudy. 'There are usually two of us on reception, but Bettina was busy helping to set up one of the meeting rooms, so I was on my own until four o'clock.'

'We understand that a business conference took place on the Wednesday and Thursday,' said Barnes. 'What time did the delegates start to arrive?'

'From one o'clock.' Trudy rolled her eyes. 'I tell you – it was bloody busy. I didn't even get a chance to use the loo until three o'clock, and that was only because Kevin covered for me for ten minutes.'

Barnes swept an upturned photograph of Clive Wallis from the table between him and Trudy and spun it around to face her.

'Do you recognise this man?'

Trudy kept her hands folded in her lap but leaned across to peer at the image. 'Yes.'

'What about a name?'

'Um, no – I can't remember. There were so many of them.'

'There's no record of his registration on the accommodation listings for that day. Any idea why not?'

The receptionist frowned. 'Maybe he didn't stay here?'

'If he was attending a two-day conference with business associates, do you know why he wouldn't stay? Was there a problem with any of the rooms?'

Trudy bit her bottom lip. 'Not that I recall. I don't know. Like I said, it was really busy. I had blokes flashing credit cards at me left, right and centre – they all arrived in groups of three or more at a time.' She giggled. 'Honestly, at one point I thought they were meeting in the car park and waiting until there were a few of them to make my life more difficult.'

Neither Kay nor Barnes shared the joke, and the woman cleared her throat before pointing at the photograph.

'Is there a problem? Has he done something wrong?'

'What time did your shift finish?' said Barnes.

'Four o'clock, when my replacement arrived. We did a handover that took about ten minutes – he never turns up early, so the handover's always done in my free time. I never charge them the overtime, though.'

Trudy set her jaw, as if defying Barnes to challenge her work ethic.

'What time did you leave the hotel?'

'About six o'clock, I think. I stopped in at the bar for a drink and got talking to someone.'

'Who?'

'A bloke. I think he might have been at the conference, I'm not sure.'

'Did you drive home?' said Barnes.

'Yes. I wasn't over the limit though. I only had one drink.'

'What time did you get home?'

'Before seven.' Trudy sighed and leaned back in her seat. 'My feet were killing me by then.'

Barnes snapped his notebook shut. 'That's all, Mrs Evans. We'll be in touch if we have any other questions.'

Kay watched the woman leave the room and waited until she'd closed the door behind her, then turned to Barnes.

'I don't understand why there's not a record for Wallis anywhere on their system.'

'Like she said, she was busy. Maybe she didn't enter his details correctly on the computer, and she doesn't want to get into trouble?'

'Maybe. Any luck with the hotel CCTV yet?'

'Gavin's waiting to hear from their head office. He'll escalate it if they don't have it authorised by the time we leave here today. He's planning on going through the recordings with someone from uniform tomorrow.'

'Okay, good.' Kay checked her watch. 'Who's that Bettina she mentioned?'

Barnes checked the list of names they'd been given by the duty manager. 'Bettina Merriweather. She's Trudy's supervisor.'

'All right. Let's have a word with her before we do the debrief and see if she can shed any light on why Wallis's record has gone missing.'

Ten minutes later, an efficient-looking woman in a similar uniform to Trudy Evans's sat in front of Kay and harrumphed as Barnes questioned her about the missing information.

'I'm so sorry,' she said. 'We've had problems with Trudy's attention to detail under pressure before. I can only assume that with the number of people arriving all at the same time she was flustered and made a mistake.'

'We understand from Trudy that you were helping to set up a conference room for the delegates. Is that normally part of your duties?'

'It is at the moment. We're so understaffed, you see. I think the hotel's popularity caught the owners off-guard. They're running a recruitment campaign at the moment, but you know what that can be like – by the time we've sifted through résumés to find candidates to interview, and then worked our way through those, it could be weeks before we're sending out job offers.'

Kay didn't comment but having sat through a number of interviews in the past week she could empathise with the woman's frustration.

'Do you have another way to perhaps show that Clive Wallis stayed at the hotel that night?' said Barnes. 'After all, his employers were billed for the full contingent of delegates, so there must be a record somewhere for him?'

The woman pursed her lips. 'I'm afraid not. The invoices are sent out automatically. Unless the client contacts us to say someone isn't coming and gives us twenty-four hours' notice for catering purposes, we simply bill them the full amount regardless. It's their responsibility, not ours. I mean, if he elected to pay for his room with his own personal credit card, that would be a different matter, but I don't believe he did, did he?'

'All right, Ms Merriweather,' said Barnes. 'Thank you for your time today.'

She nodded, rose from her seat and hurried from the room, smoothing down her uniform as she disappeared from sight.

Kay groaned as she pushed her chair away and stretched her back. 'Let's round everyone up for a debrief before we head back to the station. I have a feeling it's going to be a late night.'

TWENTY-EIGHT

Kay stirred the contents of a sugar sachet into her coffee and glanced up as Sharp entered the room.

'How's it going?'

'Slowly. There's fresh coffee over there if you want one.'

She waited while he helped himself to a mug from the kitchenette at the back of the incident room, then shuffled her notes along her desk to make room for him as he pulled over a spare chair and sat.

'What do you make of it?'

She rubbed at her right eye. 'Something doesn't add up. We've got third party evidence – the cameras on the dual carriageway at Beltring – that clearly show Clive's car on the road that goes past here. His employers confirm he attended the conference; all his colleagues confirm he was here, and he was seen in the evening at the bar. To all intents and purposes, he was staying here.' She swept her hand over the pages before her. 'The problem is, there's no bloody record of him having a room.'

'Who have you spoken to from the hotel?'

'The receptionist who was working when everyone checked in for the conference, Trudy Evans. She couldn't explain why the record for Wallis was missing, but when we spoke to her supervisor it transpires it's not the first time it's happened.'

'What about the classes Wallis took while he was here? The team building?'

'We've spoken with the staff that run the golfing green, orienteering, horse riding, and archery. The rest of them run businesses outside of their contracts with the hotel, so we couldn't get hold of them today. There's a market at the local craft centre where a lot of them have their businesses tomorrow morning, so we'll head over first thing and conclude the interviews there with any luck.'

'Any of those people come into contact with our victim?'

'The archery teacher, and the golf instructor. We interviewed the orienteering and horse riding people in order to eliminate them. We're beginning to get a better idea of Wallis's movements while he was on site, at least.'

Sharp took a sip of his coffee and let his gaze wander over the assembled documentation.

In the far corner, Debbie West sat at her desk, her laptop open as she finished updating the HOLMES database with the day's findings, the *tap tap* of her fingers on the keyboard carrying across to where they sat.

'Headquarters are making noises about reassembling the enquiry team over there,' said Sharp. 'More resources.'

Kay wrinkled her nose. 'More interference, too.'

He shrugged, conceding the point. 'I'd prefer you stayed put at the station too, Hunter – but we need a result. Something to give them to show that we're making progress. Is there anything I can do to help?'

She shook her head. 'No, but thanks. Gavin's got the security camera footage from the hotel, including the reception area. We might not have a written record of Wallis staying there, but at least we can find out if he simply slipped through the net. Trudy Evans said it was bedlam when they all arrived. Gav's taken a couple of blokes into the media suite to go through the tapes now.'

Sharp checked his watch. 'That'll take him a few hours.'

'At least. He's planning to stay late to work through them, so I've said he can have a later start tomorrow. I need this team to be alert, guv.'

'Agreed. How's Barnes doing?'

'As second-in-command, you mean? Brilliant, to be honest. I know he can be a joker, but he's impressed me this past week.'

Sharp ran a hand over his jaw. 'Still can't convince him?'

'Sadly not, and I'm not going to push it. Let's face it, promotion isn't for everyone. He seems happy enough in a support role, and I'm grateful for the help.'

'I read your notes about the candidates.'

'And?'

'I have to agree. I don't think we've found the right fit for this team yet, and I'm loath to bring someone on board for the sake of it. I'm concerned about the workload, though.'

'We'll manage. We always do.'

'True.' He glanced over his shoulder as the door to the incident room opened and the team filed in for the afternoon briefing. 'I'll stay for this.'

'No problem.'

Kay waited until he'd walked over to his office and hung his jacket on the back of the door, then grabbed her notes and made her way to the front of the room.

She stopped at Cary's desk, gesturing to the younger detective to wait a moment.

'I saw you and Gavin wandering over to the construction work at the hotel. Anything of interest?'

'Not really. The archery teacher we spoke to – Kyle Craig – said the hotel was expanding, and some old sheds and outbuildings had been demolished to make way for them. We thought we'd take a look in case we could find anything, but it's all rubble.'

'No work being done on it?'

'Not at the moment – the men who were there were contractors brought in to tidy up the site. I asked one of the cleaners about it when we were making our way back to the conference room, and he said it was all on hold for the time being.'

They hurried over to where their colleagues were waiting near the whiteboard.

Kay turned to face everyone.

'All right, settle down. The sooner we get this done, the sooner you can be on your way home.'

The hubbub dissipated until a mere murmur filled the air, then she began.

'First of all, thanks for all your help today – there were a lot of statements to take, and there's going to be a lot of information to correlate over the coming days. Gavin and PCs Stewart and Morrison are currently reviewing the security camera footage and we'll let you know as soon as we have anything to report there. We do have one statement of interest, from Trudy Evans who worked on reception the day the delegates arrived. She confirmed she recognised Wallis from the photograph we provided but can't explain why his details don't appear on the hotel's booking system.'

'User error?' said Phillip Parker from his position at the back of the room.

'That's what we're thinking. Tomorrow, you'll be sent out in pairs to interview the people who provide the offsite leisure activities for the hotel. There's a fair few of them attending this market at the craft centre premises, so I want you out the door by seven o'clock. Any later than that, and we risk getting complaints about interrupting people's regular trade. Apologies if you were planning on a lie-in.'

'That would be luxury,' said Barnes in a mock Yorkshire accent, causing a ripple of laughter through the room.

Kay waited until it died down. 'I've received

word from Harriet that her team should get the results from the laboratory on Monday, so with any luck we might have a name for our second victim. Expect a busy week ahead, because we're going to need to try to link the two victims to their killer. Any questions?'

She paused, but none came. 'Okay. Get yourselves home. I'll see you at the craft centre at seven o'clock. Don't be late.'

TWENTY-NINE

Kay threw back the bedclothes and rubbed at her eyes.

She'd been awake for the past two hours, unable to sleep and unwilling to wake Adam who was snoring away beside her with his arm thrown over his head, despite the bright sunshine that spilled through a gap in the curtains.

She checked her watch and sighed, resigned to the fact she'd only managed a few hours' rest, before she pulled on a pair of shorts and a vest top and padded downstairs.

She yawned as she pulled the coffee beans from the cupboard, then closed the kitchen door so the noise from the beans grinding and steam emissions from the machine wouldn't be heard upstairs. The clinic wasn't due to open that day, and Adam had arrived home after midnight following a call out to a farm on the outskirts of West Malling.

She'd let him sleep as long as possible.

Once the coffee was ready and a rich aroma filled the kitchen, Kay poured a large mugful and unlocked the back door.

Misha emitted a pitiful bleat from behind her wire pen, and Kay crossed the grass in her bare feet to where the miniature creature peered up at her with pale eyes.

'Morning, you.'

The goat bleated.

'I'll let you out for a bit, but stay away from the herbs, okay?'

Misha skipped backwards, and Kay laughed.

She managed to unclip the latch one-handed, then stood back as the goat tore from the pen and trotted around the edge of the lawn, stopping at different shrubs to bury her head amongst the leaves and inhale the different scents.

With one eye on Misha's progress, Kay moved back to the patio and sank into one of the chairs, sipping her coffee.

The farmers' market at the craft centre wasn't due to start for another hour and a half and the traffic would be light, so she allowed herself a moment to relax.

She'd left Debbie in charge of drawing up a roster for the interviews that had to be conducted, including the temporary stall holders who turned up each Sunday as well as the permanent leaseholders of the craft centre.

Her gaze wandered over the lawn to where a flower bed exploded with colour, a legacy from the previous owner who had been fond of roses. She made a mental note to pull the dead heads from the plants one evening after work to encourage new blooms, then glanced over her shoulder as the back door opened.

'Morning. Coffee's on.'

Adam appeared, steaming mug already in hand and held up a newspaper. 'Got some, thanks. This just arrived.'

He placed the newspaper on the table next to her, then laughed as Misha was engulfed in a sneezing fit.

'Yeah, well that's what you get for shoving your face in the vegetable patch,' he said. 'Come here.'

The goat trotted over to him and he ran his fingers through her hair to loosen the burrs she'd collected during her travels around the garden.

Kay cast her eyes over the printed headlines and

leaned forward as an article towards the bottom of the page caught her eye.

Local police no closer to arresting killer.

'Oh, great.'

'What?'

She jabbed her finger at the headline. 'Jonathan Aspley's obviously given up on getting any news from me, so he's written something anyway.'

She flicked the page. The reporter had done little more than regurgitate the known facts already presented to the press by the media liaison at head-quarters, and she exhaled.

'Okay?'

'Yes, thank goodness. I'll need to have a word with Sharp about giving the press something though. They won't wait forever, and we can't risk specula-tion with this one.'

'What time are you leaving for the market?'

'In about half an hour, why?'

'Do you mind if I come along? I won't get in the way of your team – I could have a mooch around, see if any of my clients are there. It's a popular place, and it'd be good to see some of them outside of surgery hours.'

'Of course you can come along. It'd be nice to have the company, to be honest.'

'Great.' He drained his coffee. 'I'll put Misha back in her pen, and we can get ready to head off.'

Misha bleated as he led her towards the wire fencing, and Kay eased herself out of her chair, swiped the newspaper from the table, then rolled it up and squashed an errant wasp with it.

AN HOUR LATER, they were standing by their car in a shaded area of a gravel car park outside the entrance to the craft centre, alongside a row of uniformed vehicles and privately-owned models.

The rest of the detective team milled about with their colleagues after greeting Adam, and once Kay checked that everyone was present, she turned to him.

He smiled. 'It's okay, I'll get out of your way. I'm going to go and pick up some vegetables for dinner this week. I'll see you later – good luck.'

He strode off towards the nearest of the food stalls, and Kay turned her attention back to where her team were congregated around their various vehicles and waved them over.

'Gather round,' she said. 'I'm not going to shout because I don't want anyone else to hear this.' She waited while the team took several paces towards her until she could speak to them in a low voice. 'To recap. The craft centre is only a mile from the hotel as the crow flies through that woodland over there. We're about four miles from where Wallis's amputated foot was found. Our parameters for today's interviews include ascertaining who might have come into contact with Wallis over the course of the Wednesday afternoon and evening. We know all of Clive Wallis's colleagues took part in a team building exercise with Derek Flinders who taught them basket weaving, but Montgomery Fisher confirmed that activity was concluded within two hours. His employees were given an hour to visit craft shops on site here before their minibus took them back to the hotel.'

She checked her notes. 'Debbie here has a pack for each of you that contains fresh photographs of Clive Wallis. We're using the one from his employer's website rather than the ones provided by Lucas, for obvious reasons. If you speak to anyone who can shed light on his movements on the Wednesday night, particularly where he stayed, let me know at once. Any questions?'

'No, guv.'

'All good, guv.'

'In that case, get going. The market finishes at

eleven o'clock, so if one of the stallholders on your list looks busy, you've got time to move on and then go back to them. We want to try to create as little disruption as possible, otherwise we'll have the media all over us in no time.'

She watched as they dispersed across the car park, then turned at a nudge to her elbow.

Barnes held up a manila folder. 'Care to join me? I've got a sculptor to interview.'

She grinned. 'I'd better. God knows you're not the most cultured bloke around, Ian.'

'I don't mind if I actually recognise what they're making. It's when I'm looking at nothing more than a blob of marble or bronze I fail to get excited.'

Kay laughed and followed him over to the craft centre's entry gate. 'Who else have you got on your list?'

'Travis Stevens. Blacksmith. Now, that's more like it.'

'All right. Let's speak with him first.'

THIRTY

Carys rapped her knuckles on the corrugated iron cladding of the shed at the far end of the land taken up by the craft centre. She strained her eyes to peer into the dark interior.

From where she and Gavin stood, she could hear the scrape of a chisel, then a mumbled curse.

'Hello?'

Movement at the back of the shed caught her attention moments before a voice called out.

'Come on in.'

As she led the way over the threshold, the sweet scent of sawdust teased her senses, reminding her of woodwork lessons at school.

'Over here.'

Dust motes filled the air, spiralling in the

sunbeams that shone through roughly cut windows at the top of the walls. Her shoes scuffed at splinters and offcuts of wood, and as her eyes adjusted to the dimly lit space, she noticed planks neatly stacked in orderly piles.

'Can I help you?'

She turned to the direction the voice came from. A middle-aged man towered over her, his receding hairline glinting with sweat. He wiped his hands on a towel, dirt and grease obscuring a football team's logo on the material, then raised an eyebrow as Gavin extracted his warrant card.

Carys cleared her throat and held up her own warrant card before introducing them.

'Can we have a note of your name, please?' said Gavin.

'Derek Flinders. What's going on?'

'Routine enquiries for an ongoing investigation.'

'Sounds exciting. What do you need to know?'

Carys ignored the flash of impatience in Gavin's expression at the other man's words and gestured to the workbench behind him.

'What is it you do here?'

He smiled, tossed the towel over his shoulder and crossed his arms. 'I'm a fletcher. I make bows and arrows, and I sometimes teach.'

'And you supply the activities centre at the Belvedere Hotel?'

'Occasionally, yes.'

'How often?' said Gavin.

Flinders shrugged. 'Maybe once a month. Obviously, when it first opened, I had an order from them for about twenty bows of different lengths and weights. Now I only provide them with replacements if one of the guests breaks one.'

Carys gestured towards the tools that hung on hooks from the far wall. 'What security measures do you have in place here?'

'Security measures?'

'To stop anyone breaking in.'

He rubbed a hand over his jawline. 'I lock the double doors you walked through a moment ago. That's about it, really. The main gates to the craft centre are closed by whoever is last to leave of an afternoon. We've all got a key to the padlock for those.'

'Ever had anything stolen?' said Gavin, and ran a hand over the workbench.

'No. Nothing like that.'

'Your accent. Not from around here?'

'Somerset. Grew up there. A bit hard to lose it after forty-odd years.'

'How long have you been in Kent?'

'About three years, give or take. Look, do you mind telling me what this is all about?'

Catching Gavin's glance, Carys pulled her notebook from her bag together with a photograph of the first victim. 'We're investigating the murder of a guest from the hotel, a man by the name of Clive Wallis. According to our sources, he undertook a team building exercise with you alongside some of his colleagues last Wednesday afternoon.'

Flinders wrinkled his nose. 'I remember the group, but I can't say I recall him. You say he's dead?'

'We believe he was killed some ten days ago,' said Gavin. 'Where were you Wednesday night a fortnight ago?'

'Christ, I don't know.' He rubbed his chin. 'Hang on. That's it. I was preparing for a visit from the local school the next morning. Takes a lot of work, actually – especially making sure a lot of the sharper tools are locked out of the way.'

'Anyone else here with you?'

'Travis, who runs the forge must have been here – yes, that's right. He left about fifteen minutes before me and looked in to ask if I'd be okay to lock the gates on my way out.'

Carys craned her neck and peered into the rafters. 'No security cameras?'

Flinders smiled and gestured to the stacks of wooden planks that lined the walls. 'Not much for them to steal.'

'Do you own a pickup truck, Mr Flinders?'

'No. I've got a hatchback; about six years old.'

Gavin pointed at the bows that had been placed on the workbench. 'Out of interest, where do you get the wood from for these?'

Pride entered the man's voice. 'It's all locally sourced from the woodland that borders us here. I coppice it during the winter months, let it dry out, and then over the summer I can start to make the bows.'

'Do you make anything else?' said Carys.

'Sure. Over here.'

He led them to the other side of the workshop and then stood back to let them pass.

Even Gavin was unable to suppress a whistle passing his lips at the craftsmanship before him. Carys ran her eyes over the collection of baskets for firewood, pergolas, and obelisks for climbing plants, and marvelled at the intricacy of the work.

'This is wonderful.'

'Thank you.'

'How long does something like that take you to make?' said Gavin, pointing at an ornate trellis.

Flinders shrugged, a smile tugging at the side of his mouth. 'Depends how many interruptions I get during the day. Usually three days, in between other bits and pieces. I could do it quicker, but then it wouldn't last as long, and I'd rather have my customers recommend me.'

Carys tapped Gavin on the arm and signalled they were done. 'I can take a hint. We'll get out of your way.'

He grinned. 'No problem. And if I could make a suggestion?'

Carys narrowed her eyes. 'What's that?'

'Try the hot dogs over at Alan Marchant's stall – he uses organic meat. They're the best sausages you'll find this side of Speldhurst.'

Gavin glanced at Carys and raised an eyebrow. 'It'd be a shame not to, don't you think, DC Miles?'

'Sounds like a good plan. Thanks, Mr Flinders.'

THIRTY-ONE

Kay recoiled at the savage heat emanating from the far end of the converted stable block. She blinked to get smut out of her eye and peered into the smoky interior.

A clanging of metal upon metal filled the space, and Barnes had to call out twice before the racket stopped.

'Hello?'

'Can we have a word?' said Kay, struggling to see the owner of the voice within the dark interior of the building against the fiery orange glow from the forge.

A dog padded out towards them, his mottled grey fur a stark contrast to his bright blue eyes.

Kay leaned over and automatically ruffled him between the ears, then straightened as a man approached, his sun-streaked hair tied back in a pony-tail and wearing a black T-shirt over torn blue jeans. He wiped at his brow with his wrist.

'Can I help you?'

Barnes already had his warrant card out and held it under the man's nose. 'We're investigating the death of a guest at the Belvedere Hotel and under-stand that he visited the craft centre with his work colleagues last week. You are?'

'Travis Stevens. That the bloke I heard about on the news?'

'Yes. Does anyone else here work with you?'

The blacksmith choked out a laugh. 'No – I can't afford to employ anyone else.'

Kay introduced herself, then cast her gaze over the throng of people that had begun to fill the area outside the forge. 'Looks busy.'

'Aye, well Sundays usually are. Helped along by the market, you see. During the week is a bit different.'

'How does your business stay afloat?'

'Commissions, mostly. You've met Marjory Phillips? Runs the local horse riding centre?'

Kay shook her head. 'My colleagues spoke with her though, as part of our investigation.'

'Yeah, well I look after all her horses. Plus, I

make garden gates, ornaments for fireplaces, that sort of thing.'

Barnes recited his standard introduction about their investigation. 'Where were you on the nights in question?'

Stevens jerked his head at the forge. 'Working late until about eight o'clock or so. It happens that way sometimes – when it's going right and you've got a rhythm going, it's pointless stopping.' A smile teased the corner of his mouth. 'It's not like the metal's going to sit around and wait.'

His brown eyes sparkled, and Kay was glad Carys hadn't opted to interview the blacksmith. She wouldn't get a coherent word out of her for days once she'd set her eyes on the man.

'Can we take a look inside?' she said.

'Sure. Keep your distance from the forge, though. It's hot.'

He winked, then gestured to them to follow him into the building.

Kay loosened her shirt cuffs and rolled up her sleeves to try to alleviate the sudden increase in temperature, then turned her attention to the wares that had been displayed on shelves to the left side of the working space.

'Hang on. I'll put the lights on,' said Stevens.

A row of spotlights flashed to life above the shelves, and she took a step back to admire the man's work.

Her eyes fell upon a row of knives sealed within a glass case. 'How are these secured?'

Stevens moved over to where she stood, then reached down to the right-hand side of the case and gestured to her to look. He held out a padlock affixed to a loop of metal on the side of the display cabinet.

'I've got the only key.'

She nodded, then pulled out her notebook as Barnes eyed the heavy tools that hung on a rack near the flames.

'Whereabouts do you live, Mr Stevens?'

'Out near Biddenden. My parents have a small-holding out that way.'

'And, how did you become a blacksmith?'

He pointed at the length of metal lying on the bench. 'Do you mind if I work while we talk?'

'We're nearly done. Could you answer the question, please?'

He shrugged. 'I wasn't very good at school. Actually, that's not strictly true – I wasn't interested in what they were trying to teach me. My dad was worried I'd end up getting into trouble, so he arranged for me to get a part-time job with a local farrier. I loved it. Took over his business when he retired about six years ago. Hang on – I've got to use the bellows, otherwise this fire is going to die.'

He flashed her an apologetic smile, pushed past her and strode over to the forge.

Kay and Barnes followed.

'What do you use for fuel?' she said.

'Wood. The trick is to keep the charcoal hot. Hazel wood works the best for blacksmithing, because it burns at a hotter temperature. Gives me time to do my thing and doesn't waste fuel that way.'

They waited while he tended the flames. Once satisfied with the fire, he moved away and wiped his hands.

'Sorry. The flue needs cleaning, so it can be a bit temperamental sometimes.'

'When you get visitors over from the hotel, what sort of activities do you offer them? Do they get to have a go at making anything?'

'No – my insurance would go through the roof for a start. I do an interactive talk with them, chat about the history of the place, and then show them how I make something simple like an ornamental poker or a knife, that sort of thing.'

'What vehicle do you drive?'

'That beat-up panel van out there. Has about ninety thousand miles on the clock and will probably last me another two years if I'm lucky.'

Kay snapped shut her notebook, then handed Stevens one of her business cards. 'All right. Thanks for your time. If you think of anything that might help with our enquiries, my number and email address are on there.'

'Okay.'

Kay nodded to the blacksmith, then led the way back through the converted stable block and out into the fresh air.

Barnes pulled a cotton handkerchief from his pocket and wiped his brow, squinting as his eyes adjusted to the bright sunlight after the gloom of the forge.

'So, what did you make of Thor? Did you see the serrated edges on the knives he had on display?'

'Yes.' Kay peered over her shoulder at the sound of a hammer clanging on metal once more, Stevens' silhouette stark against the flames that roared in the fire behind him. 'Escalate him to a person of interest, Ian. Let's keep an eye on that one.'

'Noted. Who's next?'

Kay scanned her notes, then pointed across the Ushaped block of buildings to a workshop at the far end. 'Janice Upton. Your sculptor.'

Barnes grimaced. 'Someone else with access to sharp pointy things. This place is full of them.'

THIRTY-TWO

A steady stream of vehicles was beginning to filter through the exit from the craft centre. Kay walked over to a shaded corner of the car park to join the group of uniformed officers waiting there.

'Thanks, everyone,' she said. 'I appreciate your time this morning. Have you all handed over your statements to Debbie?'

A murmur washed over her.

'Good. Anything urgent that can't wait until tomorrow?' No-one raised their voice. 'All right – get yourselves home and enjoy the rest of your Sunday. Morning briefing at eight-thirty tomorrow.'

The officers weaved their way back to their own vehicles, loosening ties and removing jackets as they relaxed. Kay turned to her colleague.

'Carys – have you seen Barnes and Piper?'

Carys grinned and pointed back towards the entrance to the market where a line of people waited next to a brightly painted stall, where smoke was rising into the air.

'Try the hot dog stand.'

Kay rolled her eyes. 'I might've known. See you tomorrow morning.'

'Will do, guv.'

Kay hitched her bag up her arm, then walked through the long grass towards her car and popped open the back door. Stripping off her jacket, she exchanged her work shoes for sandals, threw her discarded clothing onto the back seat, relocked the vehicle and made her way back to the craft centre.

She pulled her sunglasses off her head as she walked, cursing under her breath as her hair caught in the metal hinge on one side, then ran her hand over her hair to straighten it and dropped the sunglasses onto her nose.

Despite it being late morning, the market was still busy and she recalled Travis Stevens' comment about the popularity of the craft centre.

She couldn't prevent a smile twitching at her lips as she drew closer.

Barnes, Gavin and Adam were all standing next to

the wagon, napkins in their hands as they each demolished a hot dog, their eyes intent on their food.

'I hope you bought me one,' she said.

Adam glanced over his shoulder, flushing as he wiped his mouth. 'We thought you'd be a while yet.'

'Caught you red-handed.' She waved away the offer of the rest of his meal. 'You're all right, I'm joking. I take it they're good?'

'Best I've ever had,' said Gavin. 'The bloke who makes the bows for the archery classes at the hotel recommended them – he's got a stall here selling woven baskets and stuff.'

'Productive morning?' said Adam.

She sighed. 'Not sure. I bloody hope so. I mean, Wallis was at the hotel, there are people here that have connections to the hotel, the hotel guests are encouraged to come here and spend money to bolster the local economy…' She trailed off, overwhelmed by the task she'd set herself and her team.

'Process of elimination, guv,' said Gavin, his enthusiasm lending an excited edge to his voice. 'We simply need to narrow it all down until we've got a potential pool of suspects, right?'

She smiled – it was hard not to, such was his positive outlook. 'You're right, Piper. Process of elimination.'

Kay peered around Adam's shoulder and eyed the queue for the hot dog stall. 'Looks like they're popular. I take it you've interviewed the owner?'

'Yeah,' said Barnes, his mouth full. He swallowed. 'Alan Marchant. Organic butcher. Been running the business here for two years. Works with the local farms.'

'Any link to the hotel?'

'None.' He shoved the last of his hot dog into his mouth and licked his lips. 'I can re-interview him though, if you want?'

'Very funny. Only because you want a second hot dog.'

'You've been busted, Ian,' said Adam, and laughed.

THIRTY-THREE

Kay held the door open for Sharp, then hurried across to her desk as he made his way into his office the next morning.

The meeting at headquarters had taken longer than she'd anticipated, despite starting at half past seven. However, the woman they'd spoken with from the Kent Police media relations team had impressed them both with her proposal about how to deal with the influx of press enquiries the investigation was generating as well as using the media to increase public awareness of the monumental task they faced.

At least she wouldn't have to deal with Jonathan Aspley for the foreseeable future. The reporter had been given the exclusive to release Clive Wallis's name hours before other media outlets as a way to silence his protests.

Kay had left the building on Sutton Road with a renewed determination – they all wanted a result, and fast, but she couldn't help feeling that she and Sharp were the only ones focused on stopping their killer, rather than boosting public relations ratings.

Carys handed her a mug of coffee, and Kay checked her watch.

'You've got another five minutes before the briefing's due to start,' Carys said. 'Give yourself a breather. We're not going anywhere.'

'Thanks.'

Kay sank into her seat and took a sip of coffee, then cast her eyes over the stream of emails clogging up her mailbox and groaned.

As well as the major investigation she was leading, she was expected to continue managing other cases that had been delegated to her by her superiors. Despite the experience of the detectives she'd allocated tasks to over the course of the past week, she remained responsible for the outcome of their enquiries.

At some point, she'd have to spend time with each of them and obtain an update and provide support.

She sighed, locked her computer screen, pushed back her chair, and peered around the doorframe into Sharp's office. She saw he had his phone to his ear and signalled to him she was about to start the briefing for the day.

He raised a finger, and she nodded before retreating to her desk to gather her notes.

They were both aware that she was more than capable of managing the case on her own, but she valued his input.

As she walked towards the whiteboard, a steady stream of uniformed police officers began to wend their way between the desks, comparing notes and pulling spare chairs across to where she waited for the conversations to die down.

She opened the manila folder, withdrew four photographs and pinned them to the centre of the board before turning to her colleagues.

'Based on interviews over the weekend, Debbie and her team have finished updating HOLMES so you can review the ones you weren't present for. I want you all to do that after this briefing is concluded. These people are our persons of interest.' She pointed to the first of the photographs. 'Trudy Evans, working on reception at the hotel when Wallis would have checked in. Nothing on the system to say he stayed there, though. Could be a glitch in the system, but we haven't ruled that out yet. Next, the three people who have businesses based at the craft centre and access to sharp implements that could be our murder weapon –

Alan Marchant, the organic butcher, Derek Flinders who makes the archery bows for the hotel's activity centre, and Travis Stevens, a blacksmith. Carys and Gavin – work with Debbie and Parker on putting together a profile for each of these.'

'Guv.'

'Will do, guv.'

She glanced across to where Sharp leaned against a filing cabinet, and he nodded to her to continue.

'Gavin – how are we doing with regard to the pickup truck that was seen on David Carter's security camera?'

'I've had a response from the DVLA, but they've got no record of that vehicle being licensed in the past year. It hasn't been recorded as stolen on our HOLMES database, either. I'm working with Morrison and Stewart to ascertain if it had been regis-tered for scrap – I'll let you know as soon as I hear anything.'

Kay thumbed through her notes, then raised her head as a phone rang.

Debbie snatched the receiver from its cradle, then put her hand over the receiver. 'It's Lucas, for you. Says he's got some results on the second victim.'

'We'll take it in my office,' said Sharp, signalling to Kay to join him.

'All right, everyone. You've got your tasks for this morning. We'll have a further briefing at four o'clock today. In the meantime, you know where I am if you need me.'

She hurried over to Sharp's office, closing the door behind her and easing herself into the visitor's chair next to Sharp's desk.

He connected the call, adjusted the volume, then pulled a notepad from the top tray on his desk.

'Go ahead, Lucas. I've got you on speakerphone, and Kay is here with me. What have you got for us?'

'Okay, well as you know we didn't have much to work with to identify your second victim. The bones were so burnt, we couldn't extract DNA from any of them. However, we fared a little better with the skull. Because of the way enamel protects the pulp of a tooth, we were able to extract a sample from one of those. The results came through this morning.'

Kay leaned forward, so that Lucas would hear her better. 'Were you able to work out an age from the bones?'

'No,' said the pathologist. 'What we can tell you is that it's an adult male, judging by the size of the molars. It doesn't match Clive Wallis's DNA. I don't know if you've had a chance to speak with Harriet yet, but I caught up with her this morning and her team can confirm that there were no further victims' remains within the landfill.'

'What about a weapon? Was the same weapon used on both victims?' said Kay.

'I haven't got anything to show how each of the victims was killed,' said Lucas, 'but the same blade was used to chop up the bodies. The sawing action is the same, in that the ridges on the ends of the bones are identical for both the first victim and the second. Unfortunately, some of the bones splintered in transit – they're too brittle from being burned, so I'm unable to tell you more, I'm sorry.'

Sharp finished writing and threw his pen down. 'If you can send your report through, we'll have the team put the results through the system to see if we can get a DNA match against the records in the missing persons database.'

'You'll have it within the next five minutes.'

'Thanks.'

Sharp ended the call and sat back in his chair with a sigh.

'Without wanting to sound callous, let's hope this one has a family so we can find out exactly what he was up to before he went missing.'

Kay pursed her lips before speaking. 'I'm not looking forward to telling them how he died, guv.'

THIRTY-FOUR

Kay paced the incident room in front of the white-board and attempted to batten down her frustration.

Two murders, and nothing linking any of the county's cold cases to either of them.

She tapped the end of the pen against her chin and cast her eyes over the photographs that had been collated. Maybe she should be grateful that their killer had paused his slaughter, but it also worried her.

Someone who was so calculating, so careful to cover his tracks, would surely kill again.

But when? And why?

She threw the pen on the table next to the white-board and stalked back to her desk, resigned that she wasn't going to get anywhere staring at the photographs. Instead she decided to clear half her emails to give her mind a break.

Sometimes it worked.

Half an hour later, she filed the last of her responses, and turned her thoughts to wandering up Gabriels Hill to buy a proper coffee from the team's favourite café.

Before she could decide, she saw Gavin hurrying towards her.

'Guv? I think I've got something.'

'Is it contagious?' said Barnes.

Gavin rolled his eyes and turned his attention back to Kay. 'No – I mean something about the case.'

'Go on,' she said, and glared at Barnes.

'I was thinking about motive for anyone at the craft centre. I mean, the place is a couple of miles from the hotel and only connected by woodland, so what could Wallis and our second victim have done to attract our killer's attention, right?'

'Right.'

Gavin gestured to her computer. 'Can I?'

'Be my guest.' Kay jabbed her heels in the thin carpet and shoved her chair backwards, while Gavin moved around the desk and grabbed her computer mouse.

He opened her web browser and typed in the

website address for a local paper. Scrolling through archived stories, he mumbled a grunt of satisfaction and turned to her.

'Take a look at this.'

His interest piqued, Barnes shoved his chair back and moved round to join them.

Kay leaned across and read the article.

'Bloody hell,' said Barnes. 'There's your motive.'

'It says here that "local environmental groups have staged protests in recent weeks against the further expansion of the hotel complex, arguing that it will destroy local woodland that has held significant interest for ecologists for many decades"— Hang on,' said Kay, 'Wallis never had anything to do with ecology groups. Besides, didn't you speak to some- body at the hotel about the construction works?'

'We were told they were on hold.'

'How come?'

'One of the groundsmen we spoke to at the hotel said they'd run out of money and the owners had deferred the plans until next year.'

'Who told you about it in the first place?'

'Kyle Craig, the archery teacher, mentioned that the hotel had been expanded already – some old sheds and outbuildings were demolished at the end of last month.'

'Did you notice anything suspicious when you checked out the construction activities?'

'No – there was a pile of rubble there, which the groundsman told us had been from a dividing wall between the golf course and the outbuildings, but that was all. The thing is, I was thinking what if someone didn't want the hotel expansion to go ahead? There have already been some protests from environmental groups about the encroachment of the planned building works on the woodland beyond the boundary. If the hotel's reputation was damaged, the bookings would go down, and they wouldn't be able to afford the expansion works.'

Kay straightened, her eyes falling upon the photographs pinned to the whiteboard. 'Before we jump to conclusions, I want you all to delve further into the backgrounds of our persons of interest. Specifically, find out if any of them have links to the local environmental groups that have been protesting about the work. Get Carys and Debbie to help you let me have an update tomorrow morning.'

'Okay.'

Barnes waited until Gavin had wandered back to his desk, then leaned forward and lowered his voice. 'Killing two innocent men to prove a point about an environmental issue seems extreme, guv.'

'I know, but in the absence of any other motives or ideas, we at least need to eliminate it. Do me a favour – look into the history of the site, planning approvals, building consent, that sort of thing. See if there were any issues that arose when the hotel was first approved to be built, and whether anyone we've spoken to in the past week was involved.'

Kay wheeled around at the sound of her name.

Carys shoved her chair back from her desk and hurried over, her mobile phone in her hand.

'I think I've found him – the second victim.'

'Who is he?' said Sharp, joining them from his office.

'A man by the name of Rupert Blacklock. He didn't appear on our radar because he's from Cardiff. He's been missing for six months. His wife and kids back in Wales have been absolutely frantic – apparently, his disappearance was completely out of character. I've just had a phone call from Cardiff police off the back of an email I sent out last night asking for other police forces to check their records for us.'

'What was he doing in Kent?' said Kay.

'He's a salesman,' said Carys. 'He worked for a company that specialises in commercial kitchen equipment. For hotels.'

Kay felt a spark of excitement at Carys's words.

'Get onto his employers and get a note of his calendar and his last known movements.'

'Will do, guv.'

Kay waited until Carys had moved back to her desk, then turned to Sharp. 'Two victims. Same hotel. Too much of a coincidence, don't you think?'

'I should say so. Best you and Barnes get over there and have another word with the manager.'

THIRTY-FIVE

The next morning, Kay released her seatbelt the moment Barnes turned the vehicle into a spare parking space, then led the way towards the reception doors.

She recognised the woman behind the desk from the interviews they had conducted on the Saturday but couldn't remember her name. Automatically, she held up her warrant card.

'We need to see Kevin Tavistock, now.'

The woman paled, but she reached out for the phone in front of her, punched in a sequence of four numbers, and held the receiver to her ear, her eyes never leaving Kay and Barnes. She murmured into the phone, then replaced it.

'He'll be with you in a couple of minutes. Would you like to take a seat?'

'No, thanks. We'll wait here.'

Kay turned her back to the woman as Barnes extracted his notebook from his jacket and flipped through the pages until he found what he was looking for.

'Okay,' he murmured. 'According to his wife, Rupert Blacklock was due to stay here overnight when he disappeared. She says he phoned her after returning from dinner that night and said he was planning on having an early night because of the drive home early the next day. The alarm was raised when he didn't show up for a meeting he was due to have at Swindon at eleven o'clock on his way home. When he hadn't appeared in Cardiff by nine o'clock that night, his wife got in touch with the local police.'

'Did local uniform contact the hotel?'

'Yes, but we don't have a note of what was said. The only record entered in HOLMES is to state that the phone call was made as a routine enquiry before the missing persons information was formally released. They followed procedure and took a DNA sample from the toothbrush Blacklock left at home.'

Kay's attention was drawn to a door opening

behind Barnes, and Kevin Tavistock appeared, straightening his tie as he approached.

'Detectives. I didn't expect to see you back here so soon.'

'Thanks for seeing us at short notice. Is there somewhere we can talk in private?'

'You're in luck. We haven't got any conferences today, so we can use one of the meeting rooms.'

'Lead the way.'

Kay and Barnes followed the duty manager. He paused next to a closed door, knocked once, then stuck his head around the doorframe before turning back to them.

'All clear. We can use this one.'

While he switched on lights, Kay and Barnes took seats on one side of the table and waited for him to join them. As he sat down, Kay launched into her questioning.

'Tell me about the construction work that has been taking place at the back of the property.'

'It's all on hold at the moment,' said Tavistock. 'I don't know whether the staff told you while you were interviewing them over the weekend, but the hotel owners are waiting until the next shareholder meeting in September to make a final decision.'

'What is being built?'

'A new wedding venue. The hotel is already proving to be successful with all the activities we provide to guests. It's a new concept for this area, and it's working well – there's nothing like it around here. We're popular with the locals too, because we provide so many employment opportunities.'

Kay raised her hand. 'I'll stop you right there, Mr Tavistock.' She removed a plastic wallet from her bag and withdrew copies of the newspaper clippings Gavin had found about the protests. 'Care to explain why these protests happened if the locals were so happy about the expansion plans?'

'Oh, God. Those idiots? Honestly, I have no idea what they thought they were going to achieve.' He shook his head. 'If they had looked at the plans properly, they'd have seen that the new wedding venue is only going to use the footprint set out by the original outbuildings that were pulled down. The woodland was never going to be touched – it provides the perfect backdrop for events. Anyway, after two or three protests, it all petered out. I'm presuming someone in the group finally cottoned on to what we were doing, and decided it wasn't worth the bother.'

'Did any of the protesters harass your staff at the time?'

'Only if you count waving placards at vehicles as

they arrived at the staff car park in the mornings as harassment. They were more an annoyance than anything else. The local newspapers tried to make it appear worse than it actually was, but even they lost interest once they realised how disorganised the group was. Like I said, after a few weeks it all died down.'

Kay rested her arms on the table and leaned forward, her voice conspiratorial. 'I'm going to be completely honest with you, Mr Tavistock. I have two murder victims, both linked to this hotel. At the present time, that is the only common thread running through this investigation.'

Tavistock paled. 'You can't possibly think one of my staff members is a murderer!'

Kay said nothing and waited.

'We conduct the most stringent security checks before employing anyone,' he continued, urgency clouding his words. 'You must appreciate – with the sort of clientele we have here, our staff have to be trustworthy.'

'Well, at the moment, all of your staff are under suspicion. Unless you have another theory as to why two of your guests have been murdered?'

He swallowed, then shook his head. 'No. No, I have no idea.'

'All right, in that case I need a copy of the staff

roster for the past three months.'

'That's no problem. I'll have it emailed to you within the next couple of hours.'

'Please do. As you'll appreciate, time is of the essence.'

He leaned closer, his voice dropping to a whisper as he glanced over Kay's shoulder and back to her.

'Do you think I'm in danger?'

'Look, the last thing we want to do is start a panic,' she said. 'At the present time, it would appear the killer is only interested in hotel guests, not staff members. But, yes – do be careful, please. In the meantime, I need you to act as my eyes and ears here. If you overhear anything, or see anything suspicious, I want you to phone my direct number at once. Is that clear?'

Tavistock nodded, his face eager. 'Absolutely. I'll do everything I can to help.'

'Thank you. Then, I think we're done here for now.'

As they walked back to the car, Barnes chuckled.

'I rather think he's enjoying the thought of a killer being in his midst,' he said. 'Probably the most excitement he's had for months.'

Kay choked out a laugh. 'Ian, you can be such a bitch sometimes.'

THIRTY-SIX

Early the next morning, Kay gave herself a mental shake and squared her shoulders as the team settled in chairs and on desks surrounding the whiteboard.

Sharp pulled out a chair near the front before taking the agenda Debbie handed to him and running his eyes down the page.

'Okay, let's make a start,' said Kay as the room grew quiet. 'We've received up-to-date rostering information from Kevin Tavistock at the hotel, which includes a note of every staff member who was present two months ago when Rupert Black-lock's employers say he was a guest. Again, there is no record of his staying overnight although we do have evidence of his presence at the hotel by way of the quotation he provided to the kitchen manager.

Carys – can you coordinate the review of that list against the one we have from two weeks ago? I'm after a note of staff members who have remained at the hotel since Blacklock disappeared. For now, put to one side any staff members who left between the two murders, and staff who arrived during that time.'

'Guv.'

'We need a breakthrough, everyone, and soon.' She rapped her knuckles on the photos of the two victims. 'Although Gavin's theory about the murders being connected to the protest against the hotel expansion was a good one, I don't think that's what we have here. Something triggers these killings. It's like it's a reaction to something. So, what's driving him? Why is he killing?'

Silence filled the room.

Kay pressed on as she paced the carpet. 'Why did our killer make such a fundamental mistake losing the foot off the back of the pickup truck? He's been meticulous with how he's disposed of the bodies, even going so far as to dismember them, so what went wrong?'

'Maybe he was hiding them somewhere, and he got disturbed?' said Barnes, placing his empty takeout coffee cup in a recycling bin near the front of the incident room. 'So, he panicked. He was reacting, rather than dictating the situation he found himself in.'

'And we're still no closer to finding out where he'd come from,' said Kay, moving towards the Ordnance Survey map tacked to the wall and tracing her fingers over it. 'Our killer could have travelled from a number of directions to reach the lane where the foot was found. I mean, there are numerous routes leading off that lane, and once he reaches the main road… he could be anywhere.'

She fought down the hopelessness that clutched at her stomach and turned back to the team.

'Why did he have to steal a vehicle?'

'Perhaps he doesn't normally drive,' ventured Parker. 'That might go some way to explain why he wasn't driving with care and lost the boot with the foot in it.'

'Good point. What else? Anyone?'

Kay could sense the fatigue in the room, the way her colleagues shifted in their seats, and the defeated expressions worn by some of the younger uniformed officers. She exhaled.

'Look, I know this is hard. But let's look at it another way. Why was he in a hurry? Why risk speeding along this stretch of road?'

A hand was raised from the back of the room.

'Yes, Morrison?'

'What if he works shifts?'

'Could be one of us, then,' said a voice from the other side of the room.

A flurry of laughter lifted some of the tension, and Kay let them relax for a moment before drawing them back to the briefing.

'Very funny. Dave has a point, though. If our killer is a shift-worker, then he could have been trying to dispose of the bodies before going to work, which would explain the speed he would have needed to have been doing to dislodge the boot. Next question, then. Why is he killing? Who were our two victims to him?'

Debbie shuffled the paperwork in her lap before speaking up. 'I've run some analytics through the database, guv, but there's nothing in the information we have to date to suggest our two victims knew each other.'

Carys cleared her throat. 'Do you think he's going to kill again?'

'Yes, I do,' said Kay. She turned to the rest of the team, their faces rapt with attention. 'Whatever his reasons for murdering these men, I think we're running out of time. Either he's going to kill again, or he's going to move on, and we'll have lost him.'

She glanced up as the door to the incident room burst open and Gavin hurried towards her.

'What's going on, Piper?'

He held up a slip of notepaper as he pushed between the officers gathered around the whiteboard.

'I've heard from the team going through the CCTV images. They've got a match on the pickup truck that was used by the killer.'

THIRTY-SEVEN

Kay worked with superior detectives over her time with the police service who would never yield the floor to a junior officer, and it had rankled her. As far as she was concerned, if urgent information came to light then it should be shared and discussed as a team, rather than piecemeal. It saved valuable time, and often the ensuing discussion would net a faster result.

'Bring us up to speed, Piper.'

She gestured to Gavin to stand at the front of the room and address the assembled investigation team.

Gavin jerked his thumb over his shoulder at the photographs of the pickup truck on the whiteboard.

'Okay, well despite our first impression that the licence plates had been completely removed, Andy Grey's digital forensic team over at HQ had a go at cleaning up the images we got from David Carter – the IT consultant.'

A groan from the back of the room preceded Barnes's voice carrying over the heads of his colleagues.

'Get on with it, Piper. The short version, if you don't mind.'

A smattering of laughter filled the space, and Kay glared at them.

Gavin was renowned for his methodical work – the problem was, when he was explaining his thought processes, it often took a while to coax the information from him.

'Settle down,' she said, then turned back to Gavin. 'In your own time.'

'Thanks.' A faint blush stole across his jawline. 'So, like I was saying – Grey sent back some enhanced images, and we've managed to home in on the licence plate. Sorry, guv – could I put the overhead projector on?'

'Go for it.'

She waited while Debbie got up from her desk and handed Gavin the remote control.

'Here we go.' He flicked through a series of images, each becoming clearer in resolution as he progressed through the sequence. 'There's a small piece of the licence plate remaining on the front of the vehicle. It must've been broken when the plate was removed, and our suspect either didn't notice, or didn't bother. From that, Grey has enhanced the images further, until we see this – a partial letter and the name of the garage the licence plate was originally provided by.'

Kay held her breath and took a step closer to the whiteboard. 'Have you managed to contact them?'

Gavin turned to her, his eyes sparkling. 'We've gone one better. The garage – it's based at Ashford – has given us the name of the person who originally bought it.'

'How did they manage that?' said Carys, frowning. 'There's got to be a hundred vehicles like that around here.'

Gavin grinned, and tapped the image with his forefinger. 'There are, but that's a letter "A".'

'It's a private plate,' said Barnes, his voice betraying his excitement.

'Exactly. Grey passed on the information to uniform, who have been in touch with the Driver Vehicle Licensing Agency. The plate is thirty years old. A Mr Alan Marchant was the last registered owner.'

'The butcher from the market at the weekend?'

'The same bloke, yes.'

Kay held out her hand for the page Gavin held, and scanned her eyes down the brief report he'd printed out. 'It says here he lives out the other side of Sutton Valence.'

'The location's right, and he's certainly got the tools for the job,' said Barnes. He walked over to Gavin and slapped him on the arm. 'Good work, Piper. Looks like you've found our suspect.'

'Okay, before we go racing over there, I want a complete review of surrounding properties, roads in and out of the area,' said Kay.

The crowd moved away as instructions were passed on, and Kay nibbled at a thumbnail as she watched her team form groups that would work on each angle of the coordinated arrest.

'That's one hell of a breakthrough,' said Sharp as he joined her at the end of the room.

'He's done well. So has Grey's team.' She turned back to the whiteboard, her eyes falling on the photographs of the two victims. 'How many have we missed though, Devon? Someone like this – I can't believe he's only started killing. Look at the way he's dismembered our two victims. It's remorseless, and we still don't have a motive.'

'That might come to light under questioning,' he

said. 'It's sometimes the way. We don't always figure out why people do this to each other.'

Kay frowned. 'I know, but what's more chilling is that the statement he gave to us on Sunday seems so normal. Did you read it?'

'Yes – I had a quick read through all of them yesterday afternoon.' He sighed and gestured to the team working busily at their desks or running back and forth to one of the three printers that were working nonstop against the far wall. 'All right, I'll let you get on. Text me when you're on your way and let me have an update as soon as you can.'

'Will do. Thanks, guv.'

THIRTY-EIGHT

Kay held on to the plastic strap above the passenger door as Barnes slid their car around a bend in the road, then held her breath as the patrol car in front of them braked to take a right-hand turn.

'Jesus,' she said as her seatbelt cut into her sternum.

'Sorry,' said Barnes. He jabbed his foot on the brake once more before negotiating a tight corner that left little room for error.

Kay checked the wing mirror in time to see a further patrol car snake around the corner in their wake, the driver's face determined as he increased his speed to keep up with his colleagues.

'How much further?' she said.

'It should be down here.'

Remnants of early morning dew clung to the grass verges, a faint mist rising from a riverbed to the left of the lane lending a muted tone to the surrounding countryside.

After the briefing, the team had set out from Maidstone as the commuter and school run traffic snaked through the urban sprawl, blue lights clearing a path for their vehicles as they'd descended on the Kentish countryside.

Kay had ordered the lights off and sirens silenced several miles from their destination, worried they'd alert their suspect.

She lowered her gaze to the pages in her hand. Debbie had thrust them at her as she'd rushed out the door after the briefing to oversee the arrest of Alan Marchant at his home, and as she ran her gaze over the printed text she spotted a familiar place name.

'He went to the same school as your daughter, Emma.'

'Really?' Barnes's eyes flickered from the road to the documents and back. 'When?'

'Nineteen eighty-three. Got done for shoplifting when he was fifteen, which is why it's on record. After that, it looks like he managed to turn his life around. His dad owned a chicken farm out near Paddock Wood – there's a newspaper clipping from twenty years ago Debbie's found, and when the old man died, Marchant sold the farm and used the money to set up his own mobile butchering service.' Her hand dropped to her lap and she stared out the windscreen. 'Jesus, Adam probably knows him through the farming connection.'

'Married?'

'Yeah. One kid by the look of it. Again, he's quite successful so he's had some newspaper coverage about local Chamber of Commerce awards, things like that.'

'Any other complaints on file?'

'Not since the shoplifting, no, so nothing to indicate he's got a violent streak.'

'We'll still take it slowly when we get there though, okay? Just in case.'

'Agreed.'

Kay knew she could count on Barnes to protect her if necessary – they'd found themselves in a few situations over the years working together, but she hoped it would be an easy arrest. She didn't fancy the paperwork that would inevitably be generated by the alternative.

Nevertheless, they had both brought stab vests to don the moment they were out of the car, and given the suspect's career choice, Sharp had taken the decision out of Kay's hands and insisted an armed response unit attend and make the arrest before the property was searched.

She reached out for the radio as the GPS on her mobile phone indicated they were fast approaching the hamlet where Marchant lived.

'Okay, let's take this slow,' she said. 'I don't want to aggravate the situation by one of us letting adrenalin rule our heads. We're doing this one by the book.'

A steady chorus of affirmations reached her ears as she replaced the radio in its cradle, and she sat back in her seat, forcing herself to remain calm.

'This could be the shortest DI probationary period in the history of Kent Police if I screw this up,' she muttered.

Barnes choked out a laugh. 'It'll be fine. Stop worrying.'

His words belied the determined expression he wore, but Kay appreciated them all the same.

She dropped the pages into her bag at her feet and held on to the strap above the door once more as Barnes took the final corner approaching the building where Marchant ran his business from, then unclipped her seatbelt as he slewed the car to a halt at the grass verge.

Beyond the car, a ramshackle wooden shed leaned precariously against a barbed wire fence, while next to it a muddy driveway led to a low-slung house that hugged a recently landscaped garden. To the right of the house, a modern corrugated iron structure took up the length of the boundary line between Marchant's property and that of the neighbouring smallholding, and Kay noticed the mains power supply line that ran from a wooden pylon on the lane to a junction box in the gables.

The armed response team had burst from the doors of their vehicle before she had finished putting on her stab vest, and she watched from the safety of the lane as they split up around the house. Two members of the team knocked on the front door once their colleagues were in place at the rear, while two more men burst through the doors to the outbuilding at the same time as the front door was opened.

A woman stood on the threshold, her mouth agape at the men standing before her. She took a step backwards as the armed response team entered her house, and one of the men stayed with her as his colleague disappeared from sight.

A shout from the outbuilding caught Kay's attention and she turned to see one of the officers raise his hand to her.

'Clear – he's in here.'

A similar shout came from the team in the house, and Kay nodded to Barnes who raised his radio to his lips.

'We have authority to proceed. That's an all clear from both teams,' he said.

Kay didn't hear the response; she was already striding towards the open door of the outbuilding, ignoring the woman's protests as a uniformed officer tried to calm her in order to take a statement from her.

A chill gripped Kay as she entered the outbuilding, sending a shiver across her shoulders. She had imagined the barn-like structure to be a gloomy dwelling and was surprised to note that bright lights shone from the vaulted ceiling above her head. A familiar iron-leaden tang filled the air though, and as she fell into step beside Barnes she noticed that the door to the back of the trailer was open, a hosepipe discarded next to the back wheel.

PC Morrison was a burly figure, but she took one look at his pale face and pointed to the door.

'Get yourself outside. Get some fresh air.'

He took off at a trot, leaving his colleague to stand guard over the man she recognised as Marchant.

Ignoring him for the moment, she peered around the back of the trailer.

She couldn't stop the gasp that escaped her lips.

The floor of the trailer was covered in blood splatter; water from a hose trickled across the surface, causing rivulets to splash onto the concrete floor at her feet.

She took a step back and raised her gaze to the ceiling of the trailer. A series of hooks hung from it, but it was the sight of the bloody carcass that caused her to raise her hand to her mouth.

Despite a pervading stench of disinfectant emanating from the bucket at her feet, it was impossible to prevent her senses recoiling at the sight and smell of the dead sheep that turned on the hook.

Barnes cursed under his breath.

Marchant shrugged off the hand PC Stewart laid on his shoulder, a frown creasing his features.

'What the hell is going on? What are you doing here?'

Barnes extracted the paperwork from his jacket pocket and held it out to him. 'This is a warrant to search your premises in relation to a murder investigation we are conducting.'

As he read out the formal caution to Marchant, Kay hurried past the trailer and over to a locked chest on wheels.

'Open this please, Mr Marchant.'

The butcher rummaged in his pockets before extracting a key and inserting it into the lock.

When he raised the lid, Kay's heart gave an involuntary lurch.

Knives, mallets and cleavers shone under the glare from the overhead lights.

'Does anyone else have access to these?' she said.

'No. Only me.'

Barnes joined her and gave a low whistle before gesturing to three chest freezers that had been placed against the far wall.

Condensation ran down the side of one of them, the motors humming as the thermostats fought against the cloying heat in the outbuilding.

A sense of foreboding clutched at Kay's heart.

She ran her eyes over the lid, then glanced over her shoulder. 'What's in here?'

'Nothing,' said Marchant. 'I mean, just meat.'

She turned back to meet Barnes's gaze, gave a slight nod, then watched as Barnes took a deep breath and reached out for the handle to the largest of the three stainless steel chests.

THIRTY-NINE

'Steak?'

Kay swore under her breath and turned away from the cuts of meat packed neatly into the chest freezer, relief chasing away the dread that had clutched at her heart.

'Lamb, actually.'

'Bloody hell.'

Barnes dropped the lid back into place and stomped over to where Marchant stood, his mouth twitching.

'It's not funny,' the older detective growled.

'I tried to tell you.'

'All right. Enough.'

Kay stalked across the shed to where the two men stood, dismissed the uniformed officers who were failing to keep the mirth from their faces, and waited until the shed was quiet once more.

'The pickup that is registered to this address—'

'Stolen a couple of weeks ago.'

'Why didn't you report it?'

He shrugged. 'It didn't have a MOT certificate and it wasn't licensed. I only used it to drive around the property and the suspension was shot to pieces. It was only a matter of time before it seized up completely. Whoever stole it did me a favour, to be honest. Saved me paying wrecking fees.'

'The registration plates on the vehicle had been removed. Have—'

'That was me. I took them off a few months back. I was planning on selling them online, but the front one splintered when I undid the screw, so that was that. I was annoyed, to be honest – those were my dad's and I think I could've got a few hundred quid for them.'

Kay bit back a groan, and instead blinked to refocus.

She could hear Morrison and Stewart chattering away outside, their voices full of humour. She pushed away the thought of what Barnes would have to endure back at the station from his colleagues. No doubt the story of the botched raid would reach legendary proportions by the afternoon, but Barnes would cope. He gave as much as he took from the uniformed ranks when it came to humour, and Gavin's theory had been a sound one based on the evidence he'd obtained from his research.

She raised her gaze to Marchant once more. 'When did you notice the pickup had been stolen?'

'Wednesday night, the week before last. Whoever took it remembered to throw the latch over the gate to the paddock, though, so at least the flock didn't escape.'

Kay turned to Barnes, but he was already moving towards the exit. 'Get Stewart to tape off that gate and have Harriet and her team here as soon as possible. We might be able to recover some latent evidence, given it hasn't rained lately.'

Barnes raised his hand over his shoulder as he disappeared from sight, and she heard him barking orders to the two police constables outside.

No doubt they were losing their sense of humour rather quickly.

Despite the fact it appeared they had the wrong suspect, she would still have to ensure that a crime scene investigation team attended the property as soon as possible to rule out foul play.

As she ran her eyes over the collection of saws

and knives on a bench opposite the refrigerators, she refused to lay the blame at anybody's feet but her own.

After all, it had been the best lead they'd had in the investigation to date, and at least they could rule out Marchant as a suspect.

She turned back to him.

'Mr Marchant, I apologise for the inconvenience caused. However, we are in the middle of a major murder investigation, and I would ask that you refrain from contacting the media. Any attempt by you to speak to the press won't be looked upon favourably by my superiors, as it could alert the killer to our movements and the ongoing nature of our enquiries. Is that understood?'

The man pouted for a moment before his shoulders sagged, and he nodded.

'All right.'

'Thank you. One of my colleagues will take a statement from you regarding the vehicle theft. Please, feel free to join your wife in the house.'

In reply, he jerked his thumb over his shoulder. 'Actually, if you don't mind, I need to get on with butchering this. If I don't, the heat will get to it, and the meat will be ruined.'

Kay acquiesced, then made her way out of the

outbuilding, gulping in the fresh air as she approached Barnes.

'Don't say a word,' he growled as she drew near.

Despite herself, Kay couldn't stop the quirk at the side of her mouth. 'It happens. You'll get over it. How far away is Harriet?'

'About an hour. Stewart has established a crime scene over at the paddock.'

'Okay, there's not much else we can do here. Let's go back and brief the others.'

'I can't wait,' said Barnes, and stomped off ahead of her.

FORTY

'You've got a face like thunder.'

Kay dropped her bag to the floor next to the staircase and tried to smile at Adam's words as he peered around the kitchen door.

'It's not that bad, really.'

'You won't be needing a glass of wine, then?'

'Very funny.'

She traipsed along the hallway towards him, loosening her shirt from the waistband of her trousers and shucking off her jacket as she sank onto one of the stools at the central worktop.

He turned from the refrigerator, a bottle of white burgundy in his hand, and Kay almost salivated at the sight of the condensation glistening under the spotlights set into the ceiling.

'What happened?' he said as he poured two generous measures into glasses and slid one across to her.

'Thanks. We got the wrong suspect. I think.' She took a sip and closed her eyes, battening down the urge to groan and lean her forehead on the worktop. Instead, she ran a hand through her hair, then turned her attention to her other half, who watched her keenly over the rim of his glass. 'Tell me about your day.'

He smiled, recognising her reticence in talking about her own work as a way of coping, but playing along anyway.

'We've managed to find a new home for Misha,' he said.

'Oh, where?'

'There's a goat sanctuary just south of Maidstone and one of their contacts has offered to take her in. A husband and wife – their children are all at university, so I think they have a few animals at their small-holding near Headcorn to make up for it. Keeps them busy during term times. They're about to head off to Spain for a short break, but Misha will move in with them when they return.'

'At least your herbs will be safe.'

'Yeah, thank goodness – she nearly had the bay tree this morning.'

Kay laughed, despite herself. It was rare that Adam lost patience with an animal, but she knew how much time and effort had gone into getting the soil in their garden perfect for growing vegetables, and the herb garden was Adam's pride and joy.

'Right, enough small talk. Want to tell me what happened today?'

Kay took another sip of her wine, then sat the glass down with a sigh. 'I thought we had him, Adam, I really did. I'm not blaming anyone, I never would blame a member of the team, but everything pointed to this one person, and I got caught up in their enthusiasm. He had the means, he was in the area at the time of the murders—'

'But?'

Kay proceeded to tell him about the raid on the property that morning, her shoulders relaxing as Adam's mouth twitched, until he could take it no more and burst out laughing.

'Oh my God,' he said, wiping at his eyes. 'I can imagine your faces.'

Despite her earlier frustration, Kay couldn't help herself and chuckled. 'Barnes's face was a picture. I don't think Morrison and Stewart will ever let him forget it.'

Adam grew serious. 'So, your suspect is still out there.'

'Yes.' She shook her head, and straightened her back, easing the kinks from her shoulder muscles. 'And the more I think about it, the more I think he's going to kill again. He's too good at it, Adam. What I can't work out is how he's managed to stay hidden for so long.'

'You think he's waiting for all this to – pardon the expression – die down? You think he's going to bide his time?'

She nodded. 'Yes.'

Adam's eyes darkened. 'And, in the meantime, you're worrying about how many others he's killed.'

He reached out for her hand, and she wrapped her fingers around his, desperate for the human contact to ground her, to let her know it was going to be all right, and that she would find the monster that had emerged from the shadows.

Kay blinked, then stared at the speckled surface of the worktop, her eyes unfocussed.

'Hey.'

She raised her gaze to his at the sound of his voice.

'It's going to be okay, Hunter.'

'Thanks.'

He squeezed her hand. 'What does Sharp say about all this?'

'He's been fantastic, to be honest. I have a feeling he's sheltering me from a lot of the flak from head-quarters – they must be on edge. Of course, the longer it takes us to find the right suspect, the longer the rumour mill has to turn.'

Adam gestured at the local newspaper folded up at the far end of the worktop. 'He must be doing a good job – most of the reports in there this week and on the evening news have been general updates, nothing more. I haven't seen anything that would constitute speculation.'

'I don't think they dare to after what happened with Suzie Chambers.'

He moved around the worktop until he was behind her, then reached out and massaged her shoulders. 'I've got a great idea. It'll be quiet up the pub this time of the week. Go get changed, and we'll wander up the road and have dinner there. The change of scenery will do you good, and it'll take your mind off the case for an hour or so.'

Kay felt a pang of guilt clutch at her chest, then

sighed. 'You know what? You're right. I'm going to sit here and worry otherwise, aren't I?'

She spun on the stool to face him and was rewarded with one of his cheeky smiles.

'I don't know why all these health gurus promote yoga and stuff for relaxation,' he said. 'All I have to do is mention the pub, and you're a different person.'

She laughed and slapped his arm playfully as she slid off the stool and made her way to the hallway.

'For that, dinner's on you.'

FORTY-ONE

Patrick Lenehan checked his cufflinks, then turned to the mirror and grinned maniacally.

It had been so easy.

He couldn't remember the last time he'd had a woman like this.

The anticipation was painful; delightfully painful.

Turning away from his reflection, he made his way across to a small refrigerator, opened the door, then hunkered down and surveyed the contents.

Wine, or beer?

Patrick glanced at his watch.

Beer. And he'd brush his teeth again.

He straightened, folding back the metal tab on the top of the can, the subtle *pop* and fizz of the pressurised liquid inside teasing his taste buds.

He took a long, satisfying swallow, and belched.

Moving across to a circular table next to the window, he pressed a key on the laptop and watched as the screen came to life. He checked the wireless connection was active, then manoeuvred the cursor to an icon in the top left-hand corner of the screen and double-clicked on it.

Running his gaze over the new emails, he discarded most of them as nonsense, and closed the laptop lid. He could afford to forget about work for a few hours.

After all, he had more important things to do.

Patrick closed his eyes and ran his hand over the back of his neck, then raised the can to his lips once more, focusing on the mirror next to the bed. He reached up and loosened his tie, tossing it onto the table next to his computer, then tweaked the top button of his shirt, letting his collar fall open.

He supposed he didn't look too bad for a man of his age. If he were honest, he'd let himself go a bit in the past year but travelling from place to place and visiting clients all over the country played havoc with his life.

He moved closer to the wall and flipped the switch to turn off the main lights in the room, the bedside lamps lending a soft glow to the space. His eyes looked a little tired, yes, but maybe she wouldn't notice.

He scratched his jaw, wondering if he had time to shave, then thought better of it.

Some women found a bit of stubble attractive, didn't they?

He almost cried out when the mobile phone on the table behind him squawked.

Annoyed with himself, he moved across the room in three strides and swept it up.

'What?'

The voice at the end berated him; he was late calling.

He closed his eyes and gritted his teeth.

Truth be told, he'd forgotten, but he wouldn't tell the caller that.

He wouldn't dare.

'I've been busy,' he said instead.

He listened to the monotonous instructions; where to go, what to do, when to do it.

'No problem.'

His mind wandered, his thoughts turning to escape.

He'd become trapped, a victim of circumstances of his own making, and it wasn't something that sat well with him. He needed a way out – a way to start again and forget the past.

He had done it before, once, and it needled him that he was the one who had to leave.

The call ended with him repeating the perfunctory words that were always required, then he dropped the phone back onto the table and ran a hand across tired eyes.

He pulled out a chair and sank into it with a sigh, then reached across to the can of beer and took another sip.

He ran through his plans in his head once more. Timing was critical. He checked his watch and, realising that only a few more minutes had passed, paced the room once more.

What if he had made a mistake?

What if he got caught?

A smile teased his features at the last thought, for wasn't that part of the thrill?

He drained the beer, scrunched up the can and tossed it into the waste paper basket, then padded through to the bathroom, the extraction fan whirring to life as he flicked the switch.

He took his time brushing his teeth, lost in the motion as he paced the floor and contemplated the evening to date.

It had gone better than he had anticipated – the people he had met with had left the dinner in high spirits, and before returning to his room he had taken the opportunity to have a nightcap at the hotel bar.

That was when he had seen her.

He spat the remnants of the toothpaste into the basin and swished his mouth out with cold water before dabbing his lips with one of the white towels next to the taps.

A knock on the door jerked him from his thoughts, his heart giving an involuntary lurch.

This was it.

A predatory smile crossed his lips, and he removed the security chain before twisting the doorknob.

'Hello,' he said.

She grinned, and stepped into the room, removing the badge from the left breast pocket of her shirt before tossing it onto the table next to his car keys.

As she unbuttoned her shirt, he ran a hand over her bare shoulder, then bent down to kiss the pale skin at the nape of her neck.

'Are you ready for a good time?' he murmured.

FORTY-TWO

Peering through the slight gap between the door and the frame, she blinked in the bright light from the corridor beyond.

The soft purr of the hotel's air conditioning system reached her ears, but no sound of voices. No footsteps.

She opened the door wider and slipped through the gap, then glanced over her shoulder at the silent room within, the man's prone body stretched across the rumpled sheets, his face turned away from her.

A smile twitched at the corner of her mouth but didn't reach her eyes.

She straightened her skirt, re-pinned her badge to the front of her shirt, then closed the door and pulled her shoes onto her bare feet. Swinging her bag over her shoulder, she hurried along the carpeted hallway, paying no attention to the snores from behind other doors as she passed by and ignoring the blinking red pinpricks of light from the smoke detectors set into the ceiling as she strode underneath them.

She checked her watch. Twenty minutes to spare.

She fought down the urge to panic. If she panicked, she'd make a mistake, and that would be the end of it.

She breathed out, a shuddering breath that caught her off guard.

As she turned a corner in the corridor, adrenalin spiked through her body and she slowed her pace deliberately.

She clenched her fists, her nails scraped the soft skin of her palms, and then she held her head higher and strode towards the door at the end.

A CCTV camera lens glinted in the light from a lamp that had been set on an ornate table in the far corner, but she ignored it. It wouldn't give her cause for concern; not tonight.

She reached into her bag, extracted a paper tissue from a packet, then wrapped it around her forefinger.

Approaching the door, she jabbed at the keypad. The code had been changed earlier that day, but she'd worked it out.

All she had to do was wait, and watch.

A soft *click* reached her ears and she leaned against the wooden surface.

The door gave way under her touch and swung outwards into the night air.

Two steps led down to a paved surface, and once she'd cleared the threshold, she pressed the door back into its frame, waiting until she heard the lock reset.

The vehicle was parked close to the wall, away from the prying eyes of the cameras mounted on top of metal poles at incremental locations around the hotel perimeter.

No-one else liked to park there; in the summer, the trees cast their pollen and flowers across the paint-work, and in winter it was too far from the entrance to the hotel – she knew; she'd been caught out more than once and been soaked to the skin from cold rain that had lashed the countryside.

But, it was worth it.

She raised her gaze to the sky, a lighter hue staining the deeper blue, testament to the summer solstice that was only weeks away.

Pinpricks – stars – peppered the horizon while a crescent moon hovered overhead.

She closed her eyes and inhaled the sweet scent of the hibiscus that had been planted in the border under the curtained windows of the building, then refocused.

She waited until she reached the car before inserting the key into the lock of the driver's door. She could have used the remote mechanism, but the alarm had an annoying habit of emitting a two-tone *beep* whenever it was deactivated, and she didn't want to draw attention to herself.

She relaxed as she eased herself into the seat behind the wheel, before her thoughts jerked back to the man she'd left in the hotel bedroom.

She blinked to clear the thought, put the key in the ignition, but didn't start the engine straight away. Instead, she flipped on the interior light, checked her hair looked all right and that her lipstick wasn't smudged.

Satisfied, she snapped off the light and wrapped her fingers around the steering wheel.

Fifteen minutes.

She reached out and started the engine, a soft purr emanating from under the bonnet.

Easing the car out of the space, she kept her speed low as she manoeuvred through the car park to the exit.

The road beyond was deserted.

She risked a glance in the rear-view mirror as she

accelerated away, keeping a little under the speed limit to avoid drawing attention to herself.

He had been a bit of fun, that was all.

And, thanks to the steps she'd taken, there would be no trace of him in the morning.

No trace at all.

FORTY-THREE

Kay raised her gaze from her computer monitor and smiled as Barnes handed a steaming cup of tea to her.

'We still on for tonight?' he asked. 'Barbecue at mine, remember?'

Kay twisted in her seat to see Gavin and Carys standing next to the whiteboard, deep in conversation as they pointed at the various photographs, working through the evidence to date after that morning's briefing.

To her left, a steady stream of uniformed officers and administrative staff entered and left the incident room, their muted conversations a permanent white noise that wouldn't dissipate until the case was solved.

She sighed, knowing she was fighting a losing

battle against the bureaucracy of headquarters who would start questioning the manpower allocated to the murders.

Sharp had left an hour ago for another meeting with their superiors, promising to do what he could to keep the team together.

On top of that, Jonathan Aspley had left four messages for her within a twelve-hour period. She'd have to phone him back and give him something to work with, or else he'd lose patience and print an opinion piece that could hinder the investigation – or, worse, alert their killer to their progress.

'Guv?'

She shook her head to refocus. 'Sorry.'

'Tonight. Barbecue. Mine.'

'Do you think we should?'

Barnes pulled across a spare chair, the current owner of it nose-deep in paperwork by the photocopier on the opposite side of the room. He placed his mug on the desk next to hers and leaned forward, resting his elbows on his knees.

'Yes, I do. For a start, it's our tradition. Once a month, we each take a turn, and we've never missed one. Secondly, we need to let off some steam. Relax. You know as well as I do that's when we often get our best ideas.' He glanced over his shoulder before turning back to her. 'Just because we take a few hours out from thinking about our victims doesn't mean we don't care, guv.'

She exhaled as some of the tension she'd been bottling up left her body.

Barnes was right, of course. He'd known exactly what she'd been thinking, and she had been mulling over calling off the dinner invitation since she'd walked through the door that morning. She simply hadn't known how to broach it with her colleagues, knowing they'd be disappointed.

'Okay.'

'Good.' Barnes slapped his hands on his thighs, then stood up and took a sip of tea. 'Don't worry about food – me and Pia have that covered. I'd imagine Gavin and Sharp will bring beer, so if you want to pick up some wine on the way over, that should do us.'

They turned as Debbie approached, waving a sheaf of paperwork at them.

'Harriet emailed through the preliminary results from the paddock over at Marchant's property,' she said, handing them each a set. 'No fingerprints – she suggests the suspect wore gloves – but there was evidence of a partial footprint in the mud near the gate post. The ground is quite soft there despite the warm weather we've been having. She says she thinks it's a tread she's seen in a brand of tennis shoes, but she'll have to check into it. She'll let us know as soon as she can.'

'Thanks, Debs,' said Kay, and ran her eyes down the report as the police officer returned to her desk. 'This doesn't give us much to work on, Ian.'

'Guv!'

The shout silenced the room, and she looked up to see Phillip Parker standing at the far end, a telephone in his hand. 'I've got Robert Wilson from Maidstone Borough Council on the phone. They've found the pickup truck – it's been burned out and left in a disused yard outside Headcorn.'

Kay pushed her chair back and whipped her jacket off the back of it, signalling to Barnes as she hurried towards the door.

'Tell him we're on our way.'

KAY BIT back a groan as she climbed from the car and made her way over to where a group of crime scene investigators were already processing the burned-out hulk of the pickup truck.

When she had first got the details from Parker, her

first thought was one of surprise that her colleagues in the fire service hadn't contacted her to tell her about the blaze. Arriving at the scene, she realised why.

Despite the years since the recession, there were still sites around the county that remained abandoned – the salvage yard where the vehicle had been dumped being one of them.

Graffiti tags covered the brickwork of a concrete building that might have once been the office for the last owners and amongst the decrepit and rusting metal hulks of machinery, the pickup truck had been set alight.

She ran her eyes over what was left.

The heat from the blaze had cracked the windscreen, and it had popped out of its frame on the left-hand side. A black congealed mess pooled around what had been the tyres, the remnants of rubber tread glued to the concrete apron outside the building.

Her senses were overwhelmed by the stench of spent fuel, melted plastic, and the chemical undertones of obliterated upholstery.

Scorch marks clung to what was left of the headlight sockets, giving the impression of unseeing eyes, while what was left of the original paintwork had bubbled before cooling, leaving a mottled effect across the metalwork.

The vehicle sat at a precarious angle, and she guessed that at some point during the blaze the heat had become so intense, the shock absorbers on one side had melted.

The door to the driver's side of the pickup truck was open, and a suited crime scene investigator crouched at the foot well as he tried to collect specimens for analysis. The inside of the door had been completely incinerated, with gaping holes where plastic handles and armrests had once been.

Barnes was talking to Robert Wilson from the Borough Council and she wandered over as Harriet joined them.

'Who told you the vehicle was here, Mr Wilson?'

'The company that has been appointed administrators for the business,' he said. 'The double mesh gates you drove through are normally locked, but when one of their security people conducted his monthly check, he found the padlock broken and decided to take a look inside. It's lucky the flames didn't spread to the weeds that are growing around here. With the dry weather we've been having, it might have taken hold and destroyed what was left of the building.'

Kay wrinkled her nose. 'I think whoever did this was careful to ensure that's exactly what didn't happen. He couldn't afford to draw attention to himself.'

'I'm inclined to agree,' said Harriet. 'We'll know more once we've run some tests, but my feeling is that he used just enough petrol to destroy any evidence of his being in the vehicle, and no more.'

'You think he's an expert at this sort of thing?' said Wilson, his eyes wide.

'No. All he'd have to do is watch television,' said Barnes. 'Doesn't take a genius to set fire to a vehicle.'

'It does take someone with enough brains not to set fire to themselves, though,' said Harriet, before heading back to where her team worked meticulously through the wreckage.

'I'm presuming there are no security cameras around here,' said Barnes.

'You'd be right. Given the state of the place, I'm surprised they even bother with a security guard,' said Wilson.

Kay crossed to where Harriet had set a perimeter around the vehicle while her team worked. She watched the slow progress of the investigators as they collated what scant evidence could be found.

Barnes joined her a moment later. 'Mr Wilson has agreed to replace the padlock once Harriet is finished. Doesn't look like we're going to get much, does it?'

'No, it doesn't. Makes you wonder whether he set fire to it straight after disposing of the bodies at the landfill, or whether he kept it somewhere for a few days and then did this.'

'What you want to do next?'

'I think we speak to Sharp. I'll ask him to work with the media office to release a statement this afternoon seeking information from the general public about this vehicle.' Kay sighed. 'It's not much, but maybe someone saw something.'

FORTY-FOUR

Six hours later, Pia McLeod opened the door to Barnes's house, a wide smile on her face.

'Thought it might be you two. Come on through – Carys and Gavin are already here.'

'What about Devon and Rebecca?' said Kay, following Pia along the hallway.

'On their way. Shouldn't be too long.'

'Whatever Ian's got on that barbecue, it smells good.'

'He bought some meat from an organic butcher – says he wants to try it out.'

'Not—'

'No,' said Pia, smiling. 'Not the guy you arrested. Someone over at Linton.'

A knock at the door interrupted their laughter, and

Adam held up his hand. 'I'll get it; you two carry on. It'll probably be the others.'

As he left the kitchen, Kay turned to Pia. 'Thanks for doing this, I've been looking forward to it.'

Pia reached out and patted her arm. 'Ian feels the same way – he was so disappointed when he came home last night. For what it's worth, I think you all need a break from the case, even if it's only for a little while.'

'You're right. We could all do with recharging our batteries.'

They finished talking as Devon Sharp and his wife, Rebecca entered the kitchen.

Kay was so used to his normal workday wear of suits ironed with military precision that the sight of him in shorts and t-shirt was a shock.

'Right – everyone outside,' said Pia, and corralled them towards the back door. 'I know what you lot are like – you'll be in here talking work otherwise. Go on, shoo.'

They made their way outside to where Barnes, Gavin and Carys were laughing and joking.

Carys turned from a large stainless steel pot as Kay approached the table and held up a bottle of red wine before grinning and tipping it all into the mixture she stirred. 'Gavin had the brilliant idea of making sangria.'

'Bloody hell, Carys – you'll have us all recovering from hangovers at that rate.'

'You'll be fine. I haven't made it too strong. Looks worse than it is.'

Kay eyed the row of empty bottles on the corner of the table. 'Who's driving?'

'Gavin said he's getting a taxi home, so I'll get dropped off on the way. Late start tomorrow, right?'

'Cheeky. All right. Eight o'clock, not seven.'

'Ouch.'

'What are you two plotting?' said Sharp as he approached.

'Nothing, guv.' Carys grinned, handed Kay the wooden spoon she'd been using, then collected up the empty bottles and headed off in the direction of the recycling bin.

Sharp eyed the spoon in Kay's hand suspiciously. 'She does know you don't do cooking, right?'

'I'm hardly going to stuff up making sangria, am I?'

He smirked. 'Think I'll have a beer.'

'That's harsh.'

'How are you holding up?'

Kay gave the cocktail mixture a final stir, then

placed the spoon on a plate next to the pot. 'Okay. Frustrated, but that's to be expected.'

'Sensible answer. Rehearsed it, did you?'

She grinned.

Sharp checked over his shoulder, then turned back to her, his face serious. 'When this is over, we need to have a talk about your promotion.'

Kay took a step back, her heart lurching. 'Is there a problem?'

He held up a hand. 'No, so don't panic. It's only that if you want to maintain a hands-on role with investigations, we're going to have to come up with a plan to manage that. Headquarters won't like it.'

Her brow furrowed. 'True.'

He winked. 'Have a think about it. Help me come up with a strategy, and I'll help you avoid some of the more tedious meetings.'

'Deal.'

She smiled and peered over his shoulder as Adam approached and handed a beer to Sharp.

'Enough talking. Drink.'

Carys joined them with Rebecca and served the potent contents from the pot with a ladle she'd found in the kitchen, scooping up fruit into their wine glasses before they all made their way back to the paved area outside the back door.

'Good timing,' said Gavin, and jerked his thumb over his shoulder to where Barnes stood next to the barbecue turning over a selection of meat. 'Almost ready.'

Kay watched as Barnes used the elongated tongs to shuffle the charcoal pieces under the grill, the conversation around her ignored as she tried to clutch at the thought that had swept through her head. 'Wait.'

She strode towards him and snatched the steel tongs from his grasp.

'What're you doing?'

She didn't respond, and instead thrust the tongs into the coals under the metal grille. She turned them, mesmerised for a moment, then spun on her heel to face Barnes.

'Where did you get the charcoal from?'

'I popped over to the petrol station near work and bought it earlier today – managed to get the last bag. Why?'

'That's how he's doing it.'

Adam frowned. 'Who? What?'

'The killer. How he's getting rid of the bodies. He's turning them into charcoal.'

A shocked silence followed her words.

Finally, Carys cleared her throat. 'Care to explain,

guv?'

Kay blinked. 'It's perfect. All he has to do is get the body to the site, light the fire and let it burn. That's why the remains at the landfill site were scorched.'

'And then he mixed the remains in with real charcoal to disperse it,' said Gavin, his hand hovering over his wine glass. 'Genius. He can dump it, or even sell it. No-one would ever find them.'

Barnes took the tongs from Kay, glanced at the others, then back to the sausages and steaks sizzling above the smoking fuel. He wrinkled his nose.

'I don't suppose anyone fancies a Chinese take-away instead?'

Kay spread the evidence reports from the landfill site across the table, lined up the photographs that had been taken by Harriet's team and Barnes while she had been speaking with the excavator operator, then turned her attention to the rapt faces of her colleagues.

Their evening meal cut short, they now congregated under the bright lights of the incident room, the upbeat music from a nearby pub streaming through the panes, a stark contrast to the dark crimes they were investigating.

'Okay, so this is what I'm thinking. For some reason, the two victims draw the attention of our killer. In order to dispose of the bodies, he's dismembering them and then burning the remains. I'm working on the basis he has nowhere to bury or hide them. Barnes – what do we know about Travis Stevens, the blacksmith? Where does he live?'

'Lives alone. After we took his statement at the weekend, admin put his details into the system. His driving licence is registered to an address near Warmlake – I put it through a search engine, and the satellite photo shows it's a small cottage. Not much of a garden at the rear, and pretty isolated from the main road.'

'That works in with the theory, then. So, he probably heard from Alan Marchant that he had an old pickup truck on his property. He sees an opportunity to steal it in order to move the bodies.'

'Why burn them like this?' said Sharp. 'I see where you're going with the method of disposal – that makes sense – but why murder someone then go to all the trouble of dismembering his body and turning it to charcoal?'

Kay took a deep breath before she waved her hand over the photographs from the landfill site showing the scorched remains. 'I think it's symbolic to him. He's doing this for a reason. I can't figure out what the motive for killing Clive Wallis and Rupert Blacklock is, but to do this? He's making a point.'

'To whom?'

'I don't know. Not yet.'

She leaned forward and tapped the plans of the hotel expansion she'd obtained from Kevin Tavistock. 'The hotel expansion involved tearing down some old outbuildings here. It's too late now to investigate that area, as any evidence of other victims being kept there will have been destroyed. Stevens kills again – but he has nowhere to dispose of Wallis's body. So, he panics. He steals the vehicle and uses it to move the body to somewhere where he can burn the remains.'

Kay paused and ran her eyes over the map spread out on the table.

Carys cleared her throat. 'But surely he needs land on which he can do that? You can't just go around setting fires in the middle of nowhere, can you?'

'It's not like that,' said Gavin. 'Around here, people have been chopping their own wood and making charcoal for centuries. All you need is permission from the landowner and off you go. A lot of the farmers around here that own woodland like people to do it – it encourages new growth and keeps all the old trees from becoming a hazard for walkers and animals.'

Barnes held up a finger. 'Hang on. If you're saying Stevens is burning the victim's bodies to get rid of the evidence, where's all their stuff? You know

– clothes and things. Makes sense if he burned the bodies that he'd burn all the other evidence as well.'

Kay turned her attention to Carys. 'Did Harriet's report from the landfill site mention chemical traces for acrylics, cotton, leather, anything like that?'

'No.' The younger detective's brow furrowed. 'She said the – erm – pieces were too small to extract anything. We were lucky to get the results from the teeth.'

'Damn.' Kay took a step back from the table and surveyed the documents and images in front of her.

She knew when she'd ventured her theory that it was a long shot, but the fact that she had no new evidence to support it frustrated her.

They were so close – she could feel it.

She cast her mind back to the conversation she and Barnes had had with him at the craft centre.

Travis Stevens was in the immediate vicinity of both victims prior to their deaths, and he had the means to dispose of the bodies.

But why kill them?

What did the two men do to him that warranted their deaths?

'All right,' said Sharp. 'Based on what you've got here, I agree we should get Travis Stevens in for questioning.'

'Thanks, guv. Do you want to observe?'

'Yes. If you're right about him and he's done this before, then I want to make sure I'm in a position to brief the powers that be at headquarters that this investigation might be bigger than we envisaged. We'll have to handle the media accordingly.'

'Understood.'

'Okay. Go and get your man first thing in the morning.'

FORTY-SIX

Wendy Gibson put two fingers to her mouth and then gave a piercing whistle that sent a speckled wood-pecker fleeing from a nearby chestnut tree in shock.

'Bailey!'

An excited yip reached her ears.

She swore under her breath. 'Bloody dog.'

She checked her watch – she was already late, and the man from the plumbing company had made it quite clear that if she wasn't at home when he called around at seven o'clock that morning, he wasn't going to hang about.

'I'm booked solid for the next three weeks,' he'd said without a hint of an apology. 'It's now or never, love.'

Wendy sighed and called the dog once more. She

hated being called "love" by a complete stranger, but suspected the infuriating tradesman probably called all his female customers that, and his male customers "mate". It saved remembering all their names, she supposed.

Luckily, her boss had been understanding when she'd called him to let him know she'd be in late, even going so far as to suggest she work from home the rest of the day.

'We all know what plumbers can be like,' he'd said. 'He could be there for a while, let's face it.'

She smiled. Working for a family-owned marketing consultancy had its benefits, and she loved the flexibility of her role. No doubt she'd have to work a Saturday before long anyway, given the number of commissioned projects they were taking on, but she didn't mind.

After the divorce, she'd thrown everything at her career as if to prove to herself that the past fifteen years hadn't been a complete waste of time. Dusting off a degree in communications and getting up to speed on current practices hadn't daunted her, either.

Wendy loved learning.

The woods provided a welcome respite from the stress the broken water heater had caused her the past three days. She hated the cold, and the thought of showering under freezing water for a fourth day meant she'd accepted the plumber's extortionate call-out fee without argument.

'Bailey!'

The dog whined, and Wendy picked up her pace.

Something about the dog's reluctance to return when called piqued her interest, and she cursed as she stumbled over an exposed tree root in her haste to find out what was going on.

The wind changed direction, and she caught the distinct smell of smoke on the breeze that fanned her face.

Her heart skipped a beat, a shiver of fear clutching at her chest.

Surely someone hadn't been stupid enough to start a fire?

Her gaze fell to the long dry grass on either side of the overgrown path; if a fire took hold it would spread fast and she'd have nowhere to go.

She tried to recall the route she'd taken. Since the construction works had first started on the outer reaches of the hotel's land, her normal route had been forcibly altered. Where once she'd been able to take a short cut around the perimeter of the archery field, she now had to pick her way between thin saplings to reach a path that ran for a couple of miles and branched off halfway along its route to join a secondary path that led to the local crafts centre.

Only a quarter of a mile into her walk that morning, Bailey had taken off at the sight of a rabbit and hadn't been seen since.

Another excited *yip* carried through the trees before Wendy spotted a break between the foliage that she could squeeze through.

Shoving her hand into the sleeve of her jacket to fend off any thorns that might scratch her skin, she thrust her arms through the thin branches and found herself in a clearing bordered on all sides by tall trees.

The dog stood on the opposite side, its tongue lolling out the corner of its mouth as if grinning at her.

'Come here!' she ordered, and satisfied the dog was going to obey this time, she turned her attention to what appeared to be a large circle of metal sheeting.

Bailey joined her as she approached the structure, and Wendy bent down to clip the dog's lead to its collar in case it took off once more.

As she straightened, she noticed another overgrown path leading from the clearing, and frowned.

Several branches had been broken to make for easier egress back into the woods, and she noticed two deep furrows cut through the long grass, as if something had been dragged towards the metal circle.

Blue smoke wafted from a cylindrical chimney set into the top of the circle and as the breeze changed direction once more, her eyes opened wide in horror.

She staggered backwards and then took off at a sprint, dragging the dog with her until she paused next to a fallen log, exhausted.

She had tried to push the memory away over the years, heeding the advice of the psychologists her parents had consulted, but she would never forget the stench of burning human flesh.

FORTY-SEVEN

Debbie unfastened her seatbelt as Harry Davis eased the patrol car to a standstill on the uneven surface.

She climbed from the car, adjusted her brightly coloured vest and dropped her hat onto her head, then strode across the grass verge to where a fireman was checking valves on the side of a fire engine.

'Morning, Steve.'

He glanced up as she approached, his grim expression breaking into a smile when he saw her.

'Hi, Debbie. Pulled the short straw?'

She grinned. 'Been cooped up in an incident room for the past two weeks. I got rostered out today to cover for Harry's sidekick. Only joined us a month ago, and he's already off sick.'

The fireman turned his attention to her colleague. 'Have you lot worn him out already?'

'Very funny. What've we got?'

Steve jerked his thumb over his shoulder to where a woman with a Dalmatian dog stood talking with one of the other fire crew members.

'Someone's lit a bonfire in a glade through there. She reported it because she's never come across anything like it in the woods before, and it smells funny. Keep your distance until we give you the nod?'

'Will do,' said Debbie.

Beyond their position, the faint rumble of traffic on the road beyond the woods reached Debbie's ears, the normality of people going about their everyday business a stark contrast to the scene before her.

Two engines had been dispatched to the fire, but upon arriving at the scene the senior fire officer had assessed the situation, deemed the second crew unnecessary, and she watched as the driver of the vehicle carefully manoeuvred the enormous truck back along the woodland track to the lane beyond.

Debbie led the way towards the woman who watched the other fire crew, her dog at her side.

'Excuse me – Mrs Gibson?'

The woman turned. 'Thank goodness you're here. I was worried no-one would take me seriously.'

Perplexed, Debbie removed her notebook from her vest and opened it to a clean page while Harry crouched down and made a fuss of the dog.

'Do you mind if I ask you some questions?'

'Not at all.'

'Can you take me through the events of this morning in your own words?'

'I was out walking Bailey – we've got our usual route, but we couldn't take the path I normally follow because it was fenced off a while back and I haven't had a chance to explore an alternative until today. I don't know this area too well – we only moved here three months ago. I was rushing. I was meant to be back at the house twenty minutes ago to meet a plumber. Probably won't be able to get him back now for another three weeks. Anyway, Bailey ran off – I suppose with a new route she had all different scents to explore, by the time I'd caught up with her I found her through there.' The woman paused, her face troubled. 'I don't know what it was. Something didn't feel right – and then when I smelled what was burning, I called triple nine.'

Debbie frowned. 'What do you mean? What did you smell?'

She tilted her head a little, to try to catch the breeze, but the smoke had dissipated – the fire crew had used foam to smother the outer edges of the metal circular structure, and only a thin ribbon of blue smoke trailed from what looked like a chimney on top of it.

The woman pulled a much-used tissue from her pocket and blew her nose. 'The only other time I smelt something like it was when my brother was playing with a bonfire when he was seven, then it got out of control.' She shivered, then pointed at the metal structure. 'It smelled like burning flesh.'

Harry straightened, his eyes meeting Debbie's, and she snapped her notebook shut.

'Okay, Mrs Gibson. If you can wait over by the patrol car for a moment please?'

The woman gathered up the slack from the dog lead and hurried away.

'What do you think?' said Harry.

Debbie didn't reply. At that moment, one of the fire crew waved them over and they crossed to where the team were packing up.

She blinked as the sun's rays broke through the trees and shielded her eyes as her boots trod a path through the lush undergrowth.

The peaceful surroundings helped to calm her nerves, the green boughs of trees towering over her head.

In the distance, a pheasant cried out once before another bird responded from further into the trees.

'It's cooled down enough that we can open it,' Steve said as they drew near. 'Shall we?'

A loud knock came from within the structure, and they leapt back.

'Wh-what was that?' said Debbie. She turned to Harry for reassurance and was alarmed to note that he looked as scared as her. 'What's going on?'

He shook his head and raised his radio to his lips.

'I've got a bad feeling about this, Debs.'

FORTY-EIGHT

Kay edged around the perimeter of the wooded glade, unwilling to duck under the blue and white crime scene tape that flapped in a gentle breeze until she was told it was safe to do so.

A team of firefighters worked at the far end of the clearing, their voices subdued as they coiled hoses and carried out an inspection of the surrounding undergrowth to make sure no smoking embers had escaped their attention.

She nibbled at her thumbnail and glanced over to where Debbie and her uniformed colleague had gathered at the far end of the sealed-off area.

They appeared to be lost in conversation, the sergeant hovering close to his younger colleague as if to protect her from further distress.

Kay averted her eyes to give them some privacy.

Each and every one of them had a different coping mechanism that developed over time and exposure to different situations they were confronted with on the job, but if this was the first time Debbie had seen a burned body, it would likely stay with her for a long time, if not forever.

The woman's face was still pale as she walked over to Kay.

'He must've died in agony,' she said, and wiped at her eyes. 'He was curled up into the foetal position, guv. His hands were like claws clutching at his chest.'

Kay reached out and placed her hand on the woman's arm. 'Debs, that happens naturally to a human body when it burns. Hopefully Harriet will confirm it, but chances are he was dead before he was placed inside.'

Debbie blinked. 'You think so?'

'I do, yes.' She peered over the woman's head to where Harriet was speaking with the leader of the fire brigade team. 'I don't think our killer would have been able to get him into that metal circle otherwise. I think this was a disposal method, not how he murdered him.'

'So, what made the sound we heard?'

'It was probably caused by the bones constricting in the heat.'

Debbie shuddered. 'I've never had a burned one before. First time.'

Kay squeezed her arm before letting go. 'Are you going to be okay?'

'Yeah, I think so. Thanks.'

'You know where to find me if you need me.'

'Thanks, guv. I appreciate it.'

They broke off their conversation as one of Harriet's assistants approached the tape and waved Kay closer.

'Back in a minute,' she said to Debbie, and hurried across to the CSI team member.

To her right, Barnes strode to catch up with her, his mobile phone held to his ear.

'Carys confirms there's a patrol car on the way to arrest Travis Stevens.'

Kay clenched her fists at her sides. She'd been too late to save the man whose remains lay in the kiln, and it would haunt her, she knew. 'Okay, thanks. Join me?'

He finished the call, tucked the phone into his shirt pocket and donned the plastic coveralls Kay handed over to him from a box at the perimeter. They both signed the clipboard Harry Davis held out to them, then moved into the sealed-off area.

'You ready for this?' Kay murmured under her breath as she eyed Harriet's team milling about, waiting for them.

'As I'll ever be,' said Barnes. 'Debbie all right?'

'She says she's okay. I'll keep an eye on her.'

He gestured to the firefighters, who were now traipsing back to their vehicle. 'Did they say how they put it out? I can't imagine Harriet will be pleased if they soaked the evidence.'

'Apparently the structure has holes all around the outside, near the bottom. All they had to do was seal those and the fire quickly died once it was starved of oxygen. Harriet was asked to come here at the same time as you got a call, so she was able to help supervise the preservation of the body.'

They fell silent as the long grass swished against their legs, and Kay ran her eyes over the scene before her as the woman approached.

'What've we got, Harriet?'

The lead crime scene investigator pulled her mask down from her face while her team began to clear the contents of the metal structure.

'Okay, well despite the shrinkage in the bones caused

by the fire, I'd say it's an adult male, judging by the size of the body. He's been in here a while; maybe six hours.' She gestured to the corrugated iron circle. 'And, before you two get too excited, despite being in one piece this one's not going to give up his secrets easily,' said Harriet. She beckoned them towards the metal circle.

Kay swallowed and held her breath. The last thing she wanted to do was look, but she knew from experience that she'd have a better understanding of the killer's methods if she tried to learn as much as possible while at the crime scene.

'You said "he"?'

Harriet nodded. 'Plus, I don't think a woman would've been able to lift the victim over the edge of this, let alone drag him through the undergrowth to get here.'

'Have you found drag marks?' said Barnes, craning his neck to see beyond the tape at the back of the crime scene.

'Through there. That area we've taped off indicates someone walked here carrying a large weight – the grass is trampled down to the bare earth. The structure has been here a while – it's designed so that one person can up-end it and roll it into position but we haven't found any evidence of that being done lately.

'Footprints?' said Kay, unable to hide the trace of excitement in her voice.

'Sorry, no – the ground is too hard from the lack of rain we've had this month.'

Harriet paused next to the metal circle and indicated they should look inside.

Kay exhaled, then peered over the jagged metal edge.

The circle itself came up to her chest and was a wide structure that yawed before her.

She let out a groan.

Curled up in a foetal position, exactly how Debbie had described, were the burned remains of an adult male.

As the fire had cooled, his bones had cracked and splintered apart, leaving a jigsaw-like impression of a human. Kay turned away, fighting down bile.

'Did he die here?'

'No,' said Harriet. She climbed a step-ladder that had been placed against the structure, then leaned over and pointed to the victim's skull. 'Blunt trauma wound here. Obviously, we'll have to wait for Lucas to confirm it, but my best guess is this was the killing blow.'

'So, he's trying to burn the body to hide the evidence,' said Kay.

'Not so fast,' said Harriet. 'This fire was never going to reach the sort of temperature required to completely destroy a body.'

'What do you mean?'

'Look at the way the body has been placed on top of everything else in here. All right, it's burned down and reduced, but the fire was started with dry brushwood, then it looks like tree branches were added – your killer has stacked those up in such a way that the fire would burn slowly. I'll have the wood remains sent away for analysis, but the fact there are still charred remains here suggests to me that it's a hardwood such as hazel.'

Barnes stepped away from the metal structure. 'What is this thing, anyway? A compost heap?'

'No, it's a kiln – Charlie over there says he used to see them all the time when he was a kid.'

'A kiln?' said Barnes. 'Like, with pottery?'

'No, for making charcoal,' said Harriet. 'It's been reduced to a cottage industry around these parts now, but it was once a way for locals to make some money during the spring and summer months. They would cut down the wood to manage it and keep new growth sustained, while selling on what they produced – either using the wood for fencing or turning it into charcoal. Someone knows what he's doing.'

FORTY-NINE

Kay glanced up from the notes she'd placed in a file to see Sharp advancing towards her, Barnes and Carys in his wake.

'Are you ready?' said Sharp.

'Yes. Sergeant Hughes booked him in a couple of hours ago – uniform picked him up when we were at the crime scene. He hasn't said anything; I think he might be in shock.'

'Who's his solicitor?'

'A chap called Hargreaves from a firm over at Ashford.'

'All right. I'll be observing, and Carys can take additional notes. I don't want this one getting away, Kay. We have to stop him, and we have to stop him now.'

'Understood, guv.'

She waited while Sharp, Carys and Gavin proceeded to enter the observation room, gave them a few moments to switch on the monitors that provided them with a live link via camera to the interview room, then turned to Barnes who nodded and swiped his card across the lock.

He held open the door for her, then made his way across to the recording equipment before taking a seat beside her. Once the formal caution had been read out, Kay opened the file before her and raised her gaze to Travis Stevens.

Sweat formed at his hairline, and a deep crease mottled his forehead as he picked at a scab on the back of his hand. His eyes darted to the door, then back to her.

'When we spoke to you last week, you stated that you'd been working late on the nights of Wednesday and Thursday. What did you do when you left the craft centre?'

'Nothing much. I was tired, so by the time I got back home I just watched a bit of television.'

'What time did you get home?'

His brow puckered further and he rubbed at the back of his hand a final time before leaning back in his seat and crossing his arms over his chest. 'Well, it only takes half an hour or so, so I guess it must've been about eight-thirty, quarter to nine, something like that.'

'The charcoal you use at the forge. Where do you get it from?'

'I make most of it myself in the spring. It's too expensive to buy during the summer because everyone around here has a barbecue the moment there's a sniff of a good day. I'm usually too busy at the craft centre during the summer anyway, so I don't get a chance to make any then.'

'Where do you make it?'

'Why do you want to know? What's going on?'

'Answer the question, Mr Stevens.'

He glanced at his solicitor, but the man only raised his eyebrows in response.

'There's a bit of private woodland over near my parents' place at Biddenden. The owner lets me coppice what I need after winter – saves him a job.'

Kay paused to check her notes. 'That would be the woodland that backs onto the A262?'

'Yeah.'

'What do you use to make the charcoal?'

'A kiln, of course. Me and my dad made one a few years ago out of some old corrugated iron sheeting he had.'

'What happens to the kiln when you're not using it?'

'I don't know. I just leave it there. We used to roll it onto a trailer and take it back to my parents' place after each burn, but that was a pain to be honest.'

'Do you have any other kilns in the area?'

'No – why would I?'

'When was the last time you went there – to the woods at Biddenden?'

His brow puckered, and he rubbed a hand over his jawline. 'Must've been the end of April. Yeah, April. I did one final burn to get me through to the end of August.'

'Where do you store your charcoal?'

'With a mate of mine.'

'Why not keep it at the forge? Wouldn't that make sense?'

He shrugged in response, lowering his eyes.

'We'll need a name.'

Kay waited while Barnes scribbled the details into his notebook, then turned her attention back to Stevens.

'Where were you between the hours of noon yesterday and nine o'clock this morning?'

'At home.' Hope flashed in his eyes. 'You can ask my sister and her husband. They stayed with me because they were driving down to Ashford to catch the train to France this morning. They left just before your lot turned up.'

'Phone number?'

He recited a mobile number from memory, and Kay let her gaze wander to the camera fixed to a bracket in the ceiling behind Stevens, before she turned to Barnes and nodded.

'Interview suspended.'

She pushed her way out the door and paced in the corridor while Barnes shut it behind them. Sharp strode from the observation suite.

'What do you think?' he said.

She ran a hand over the back of her neck. 'I'd like to keep him for the full increment of hours. Gives us time for the team over at the forge to process the scene and come back to us.'

'Is it him, do you think?'

'He's lying about something, that's for certain. He was being evasive during the interview.'

'I'm inclined to agree,' said Barnes. 'Maybe we're looking for two killers, not one, and he's protecting someone.'

'All right,' said Sharp, checking his watch. 'We'll sign off the paperwork to hold him in custody for now. That gives you another few hours to come up with something.'

'Hold on.' Carys appeared at the door to the observation suite and held up a note. 'I've phoned the number he provided. His alibi checks out – his sister and brother-in-law travelled over from Worcestershire two days ago. Apparently, they all had dinner together at Stevens's place last night before they headed off to Ashford at eight o'clock this morning.'

Kay glanced at Barnes, then back to Sharp. 'He's not our man then. He's telling the truth. There's no way he could've got over to the woods and back home in that timeframe.'

'Do you think someone else knew about his kiln?' said Carys.

'Must've done.' She spun on her heel. 'Barnes – with me.'

She shoved open the door to the interview room, stabbed the "record" button, and swung around to face Stevens.

'Who knows about the kiln?'

'Eh?'

'You heard me. Who else uses the kiln?'

'I don't know.'

Barnes glared at him. 'Another victim was discovered this morning, Travis, burned to a crisp in a charcoal kiln. For the life of me, I can't understand why you're being so evasive if you say you're innocent. You know something, and unless you want me to charge you with obstructing the course of justice, talk.'

The man's solicitor cleared his throat, and when his client turned to face him, he raised an eyebrow and jerked his head in the direction of the two detectives.

Stevens paled, but managed a slight nod. 'All right. Look, when your lot turned up, I panicked, okay? I-I grow a small amount of marijuana out the back of the forge.' He raised his hands. 'I don't sell it. It's for my own use only. It helps with the arthritis in my wrists. If I can't work, I don't earn anything.'

Kay exhaled, and she shook her head in wonderment. 'Why on earth didn't you tell us this before?'

'Like I said, I panicked. I can't afford to lose my business. Besides, I'm not the only one who makes charcoal around here. If I run out, I have to buy more – I haven't got time to do a burn over the summer months because that's when I do most of my work.'

Kay's eyes narrowed. 'Who do you buy your charcoal from?'

'Derek Flinders. Why?'

FIFTY

Carys held her head in her hands, her complexion a sickly pallor as Kay brought the afternoon briefing to a close.

'I should've known. I should've picked up on it when we spoke to him.'

Kay noticed Gavin wore an equally distressed expression.

The revelation that Derek Flinders could well be their main suspect had shocked them all, not least the two detectives who had interviewed him as part of the initial investigation at the craft centre two weeks ago.

'Jesus,' said Gavin, and ran a hand over his spiky blonde hair. 'He's killed someone else since then. We could've stopped him. I didn't even consider that he might make charcoal out of the wood he coppices. I thought he only made the archery supplies and craft stuff we saw in his workshop.'

'Stop it right there,' said Kay, and leaned against a desk beside them. She eyed them both before continuing. 'We're dealing with a killer who has sociopathic tendencies. You've done the same training as me, and you know how devious someone like this can be. I've read the witness statement you took from him, and you did nothing wrong. The questions you asked were sound, and his responses gave nothing away. He's intelligent, and he fooled us all.'

She raised her gaze over Gavin's shoulder as Sharp joined them.

'Kay's right,' he said. 'Learn from the experience, but don't let it fester in your minds. We need to focus, and we need to formulate a case against him before we bring him in for questioning.'

'Guv,' said Carys, her eyes downcast.

'Come on,' said Kay, rising to her feet. 'Like I said in the briefing, we need to retrace our footsteps with that interview and check out his employment history. Gav – can you phone the bloke that manages the office at the craft centre and find out if Derek Flinders is there today?'

'Will do.'

Kay turned back to Carys. 'Like Sharp said – get

back in the saddle. I need you to go through the database again to find out if there are any similar cases to this around the country. Widen the original search we conducted last week. Someone like this has had practice, I'm sure of it.'

'Guv.'

Satisfied her colleagues' work would keep their minds occupied for a while, Kay strode back to her desk with Sharp in tow.

His phone began to ring as they drew near, and he broke away to hurry into his office to answer it.

'Probably the media office,' he called over his shoulder.

Kay sank into her chair and turned her attention to Barnes who sat across from her. 'Ian – how is the analysis from this morning's crime scene coming along?'

'Surprisingly well preserved,' he said, glancing up from his computer screen. 'Harriet's team have sent a preliminary email saying they've retrieved what looks like remnants of a leather wallet – small pieces, mind – and a metal belt buckle. Two gold rings were found within the kiln, too. Possibly a wedding band and a signet ring.'

Kay exhaled, the sobering reality that she would

have to inform a woman that her husband had been murdered plaguing her thoughts.

'Anything else?'

Barnes shook his head. 'They're still processing the scene.'

Kay rubbed her temples while she tried to concentrate. They were so close now – all the evidence was starting to point to Flinders as their killer but again, she had no idea what was motivating him.

She reached out for her computer mouse, wiggled it to bring her computer screen to life, and pulled up the transcript of the interview Carys and Gavin had conducted at the craft centre with the man.

She'd been right – there had been nothing to suggest anything suspicious in the man's responses, and neither detective had noted any reluctance to answer their questions, but she sighed as she read the final sentence.

'You all right?'

She glanced up at Barnes's voice. 'According to these notes, it was Flinders who recommended the hot dogs from the butcher's van at the craft centre.'

'Bastard. He set him up.'

'Put us right off his scent for a while, didn't it?'

Gavin hurried over to them. 'I've spoken to the craft centre. They haven't seen Flinders for over forty-eight hours. No-one knows where he is, and he's not answering the mobile number we took from him.'

'Do you want me to put out an alert for him?' said Barnes.

'Yes,' said Kay. 'All ports as well. Do you have a home address for him, Gav?'

'Already passed it on to uniform.'

'Good. If he's not there, tell them to wait.'

'Will do.'

He shot off towards his desk.

'So,' Barnes continued. 'He recommends the hot dogs and has the audacity to steal the man's pickup to move two bodies – or parts of them.'

'Get onto Alan Marchant and ask him if he's had a run in with Flinders lately, Ian. It might be nothing, but maybe there's a connection there we haven't yet uncovered.'

Carys raised her hand. 'I've already got a result. On the database, I mean.'

'Go on.'

'I extended the search beyond Sussex, Surrey and the City – about four years ago, similarly burned body parts were found scattered at a disused construction site in Bristol. Teeth were used to identify a salesman from Plymouth who had gone missing. I've also got two more missing men who were last seen in Bristol five years ago, one from Nottingham and one from Bedford. No remains have ever been discovered.'

Kay frowned, then turned to Barnes. 'Bristol? Where have I heard that before?'

'Hang on.'

Barnes grabbed his notebook and flipped through the pages. 'Here we go. Trudy Evans. When we spoke to her, she said she arrived at the hotel three and a half years ago. She'd been in Bristol before that.'

'Bring her in,' said Kay. 'Now.'

FIFTY-ONE

When Kay walked into interview room two ahead of Barnes, her first impression was that Trudy Evans appeared petrified.

Her eyes wide, she watched the two detectives as they settled into their seats, her breath escaping in gasps while a trickle of perspiration at her hairline caught the light from the fluorescent strips in the ceiling.

Barnes completed the formal caution, and Kay turned to the woman.

'Trudy, do you need a glass of water or anything before we begin?'

'N-no.'

Kay's glanced at the woman sitting beside Trudy,

a duty solicitor from one of the local firms based on Mill Street, and raised her eyebrow.

The solicitor gave a subtle shake of her head.

Obviously, she was concerned about her client's nerves too, but she remained poker-faced nonetheless. It probably didn't help that the solicitor, like her client, had been roused from her slumber half an hour before midnight and was now trying to stifle a yawn.

'All right. Let's begin by you telling us in your own words what happened the day Clive Wallis turned up at the hotel with his colleagues.'

'I've already told you,' said Trudy, her brow creasing as she looked from Kay to Barnes.

'This is now a formal interview,' said Barnes. 'We need you to clarify on record what you told us in your statement, because we have further questions.'

'Oh. Okay. Um, so yeah – everyone from the company turned up at more or less the same time that Wednesday. Like I said, it was bedlam.'

'Can you confirm what time they started arriving?'

'About one o'clock.'

'Did you leave the reception desk at any time during your shift?'

'Kevin finally remembered I'd need a toilet break.

That was about three o'clock. I was only gone for ten or fifteen minutes.'

'Which toilets in the hotel did you use?'

Trudy rolled her eyes. 'The ones next to reception, of course. They're the nearest.'

Barnes slid the photograph of Clive Wallis across the table. 'Please confirm for the record – do you recognise this man?'

'Yes. He's the one you asked me about.'

'And where have you seen him before?'

'He was with the others. When they checked in.'

'Have you been able to recall his name since we last spoke with you?'

'No – sorry. I see so many guests, I don't remember all their names. Not unless they stand out – like, if they're rude or extra polite.'

'Did you see him at any other time between Wednesday afternoon and Friday morning?'

Trudy shook her head.

'You need to answer for the recording, please.'

'No – that was the last time I saw him alive.'

'A strange turn of phrase,' said Barnes. 'Care to explain?'

'I didn't kill him,' Trudy spluttered. Her eyes opened wide when neither of them responded, and she turned to her solicitor. 'They think I killed him?'

The woman next to her remained impassive but made a calming gesture with her hand, and her client turned back to face the detectives.

Kay flipped open the folder in front of her and cast her eyes down the page. 'You moved here from Bristol three years ago. Why was that, Trudy?'

'Fancied a change, to be honest.'

Kay's senses picked up on the phrasing of the woman's answer, and she raised her gaze as she pushed a newspaper clipping across the table towards her. 'It appears that while you were in Bristol, two men went missing. From the hotel you worked at.'

'What?' Trudy picked up the clipping, her eyes scanning the words while her face paled further. Eventually, she dropped it back to the table, her hands shaking. 'I never killed no-one. You have to believe me.'

'Why did you come to Kent?'

'I don't know. I was bored where I was.'

'The hotel where these men went missing.'

'Yeah. It was a conference centre in the city. The pay was all right, I suppose, but it's a pain getting around the city – and expensive to rent. Prices keep going up, y'know? When the opportunity came up to take on a job with the company's new hotel in Kent, I figured it was a good excuse to get out.'

'How did you apply for the role?'

Trudy's eyes lit up, and a smile reached her lips, her nerves forgotten for a moment as she sat up straighter. 'I didn't apply – I was headhunted,' she said, a note of pride filling her voice, colour returning to her cheeks.

'By whom?'

'Bettina. The supervisor I report to now. We'd worked together in Bristol until she left three months before me to help launch the hotel here. It's the company's flagship venue, and they wanted her to be on board right at the start. Once she got settled, she phoned me up and offered me the job. I wasn't going to turn it down, was I?'

Kay glanced at Barnes, who wore the same perplexed expression she was sure clouded her own features. He recovered quicker than her though.

'How long have you known Bettina Merriweather?' he said.

Trudy shrugged. 'About six years, I suppose. She recruited me in Bristol – I'd had enough of working in pubs and fancied a change. The money was better at the time too. I was single when the opportunity here came up, so I grabbed it.'

Kay signalled to Barnes, and he leaned towards the recording equipment.

'Interview paused at eight oh seven.'

'What do you think?' she said, once they were outside and he'd closed the door to the interview room behind them.

He scratched his chin. 'A bit convenient, her following her boss a few months after she'd moved to Kent, wasn't it?'

'Maybe. But what if Bettina was the one who wiped Clive Wallis's name off the system? She'd have the ability to do so, being Trudy's supervisor, wouldn't she?'

'So, you mean Trudy's telling the truth – she did enter everyone's names onto the system, but it was her boss who deleted the information?'

'Yes.' Kay tapped the manila folder against her leg and contemplated the threadbare carpet.

'Guv?'

She lifted her head at the sound of running footsteps to see Gavin barrelling along the corridor towards her.

'What's up?'

'We just got a call from the uniformed patrol that went to Derek Flinders' house. He's not there, but his wife is.'

'Okay. And?'

'Kay, his wife is Bettina Merriweather.'

FIFTY-TWO

Kay pulled out a chair in front of the slight woman who sat next to a dour duty solicitor, then dropped a manila folder onto the desk, the documentation landing with a *slap* that made Bettina Merriweather jump in her seat and raise her chin.

Her solicitor frowned at Kay, his yellowing moustache disguising the curled lip she knew would be aimed at her for the late night. She glared back at him, waited until Barnes had started the recording and incited the formal caution, then began.

'Please state your full name and address for the record.'

'Bettina Merriweather. Rosewell Cottage, Sutton Valence. Where's my son? He's only fifteen.'

'Our uniformed officers spoke to your neighbours. Mark's with them at the moment.'

'Okay.'

'Where do you work?'

'The Belvedere Hotel.'

'How long have you worked there?'

'Three years.'

'What does your role there entail?'

'I'm responsible for managing the reception staff, providing overall coordination for the corporate events, and once the wedding venue is complete, I'll be managing that as well.'

'Why don't you use your husband's surname?'

'It was what we agreed when we got married. I liked my maiden name, and he didn't mind.'

'What's your marriage like, Bettina?'

'What?' The woman's jaw dropped, and she leaned back in the hard plastic seat. 'What's that got to do with you?'

'Answer the question.'

'It's… it's—' The woman's eyes welled with tears. 'It's crap, actually.'

'Does he beat you?'

'God, no.' Bettina reached across and plucked a tissue from the box near the recording equipment and blew her nose before continuing. 'It's over, that's all.

Not that Derek will accept it. I've wanted to leave him for years, but until Mark's old enough to look after himself, I can't.'

Kay said nothing and clasped her hands on the desk while she waited for the woman to continue.

Eventually, Bettina's shoulders slumped.

'Derek is – God, how to explain? I worry what he'll do if I leave him. I'm trapped – if I left and he did something stupid, I'd feel so guilty. I'd blame myself.'

'What do you mean by "something stupid"?' said Kay.

A shuddering breath escaped Bettina's lips. 'He doesn't like it if another man even just looks at me. If I mention any of my friends' husbands in conversation, he loses his temper. Not that we have many friends anymore.'

'Why not?'

'He threatened one of them, about a year ago. We were at someone's birthday party at that big pub on the High Street. One of the mums from Mark's school. I got talking to her husband. All he did was compliment me about the earrings I was wearing. Derek overheard, walked across to where we were talking, and punched him. He and his wife – and the rest of them – haven't spoken to us since.'

'Were charges brought?'

'No.'

'What did Derek have to say about it?'

'He said the bloke deserved it, and that he didn't want me to socialise with those sorts of people. I hardly go out now. It's stupid – I don't even like him touching me anymore. All we seem to do is argue. I can't even remember why I fell for him in the first place,' she said, and dabbed at her eyes. 'Pathetic, isn't it? All I wanted was to feel loved.'

'Is that why you started having affairs with hotel guests?'

Bettina gasped, dropping her hands to her lap as she stared at Kay. 'How did you—'

'It was you who deleted the guests' names from the computer system, wasn't it?'

The woman choked out a sob, then nodded.

'I need to you speak for the record, Bettina.'

'Yes,' she croaked. 'It was me.'

'Why?'

'I can't afford to lose my job. My son has to have special lessons twice a week to help with his school-work so he doesn't fall behind, and Derek never makes enough to cover the costs.'

'Tell me what you did.'

Bettina sniffed, then swallowed and leaned

forward, folding her arms on the desk. 'I never slept with the men who paid by personal credit card – that would've raised a bloody big flag on the system. Only the ones I fancied who had their bills paid for by their employers. It didn't matter then.'

'Why blame Trudy?'

'Because she's messed up before. I'm always covering for her.'

'Does Derek know about your affairs?'

Bettina's eyes widened. 'He – he can't. I've been so careful.'

'Are you sure?'

'Yes. I mean – he'd have said something, wouldn't he?'

'What do you tell him? He must be aware of your shifts, so how have you managed to fool him?'

'I tell him I have to work late. I never slept with anyone on my early shifts – too many people around. We need the extra money so he's never questioned my overtime.'

'What if one of your colleagues told him?'

'What? No – they wouldn't. They don't know what I've been doing, do they?'

'What do you think he'd do if he found out?'

'I don't know.'

'I think you do.'

Kay took a deep breath and flipped open the folder, the cover warm from the freshly printed pages inside. She extracted a photograph and spun it around to face the other woman.

'Do you recognise these rings?'

Bettina's eyes widened before she raised a shaking hand to her mouth. She nodded.

'What's his name, Bettina?'

Fat tears rolled down the woman's cheeks, and she wiped at them with the palm of her hand before taking a shuddering breath.

'Patrick Lenehan. I met him the other night. He said he had an early flight to Cork. He had a taxi turning up at three o'clock yesterday morning to take him to the airport.'

'Which airport?'

'I don't know. I didn't ask him.'

'Which taxi company?'

'Alpha Limousines. I booked it for him.'

'Interview terminated at one forty-five. Barnes, with me.'

Kay shoved her chair back and raced across to the door, then flung it open and nearly collided with Sharp as he rushed from the observation suite with Carys in tow.

'We need to get onto the taxi company and find

out if he was collected from the hotel,' she said.

'On to it, guv,' said Carys, and stabbed the details into her phone.

'Find out if he made that flight, too,' Kay added. 'It'll be one of the airlines out of Luton.'

Carys gave a thumbs up in reply and moved to the end of the corridor as her call was answered.

Kay paced the tiled floor, unable to keep still. 'I've gone through all the interviews that were conducted at the hotel and the craft centre, guv – how the hell did I miss that she and the archery supplier were married?'

'Calm down, Kay. We all missed it, because neither of them volunteered the information. Makes you wonder how long the marriage has been over, doesn't it?'

'For her, maybe,' said Kay, shaking her head. 'I don't think it is for him.'

'You think her husband killed Lenehan and that's who was found burned in the kiln?' said Sharp, his grey eyes concerned.

'I do, yes. From what she's told us, I'm willing to bet he's well aware of her affairs. I'm also willing to bet that rather than confront her, he's killing the men she sleeps with.'

'Guv!'

Sergeant Hughes hurried towards her.

'What is it?'

'Thought you should know – a report of a stolen vehicle came through earlier this morning. I noticed the address when I booked in Mrs Merriweather and thought I'd seen it before. It's a four-door silver saloon.'

Kay took the note from his outstretched hand and ran her eyes down the page. 'Bloody hell. She reported her car as being stolen this morning.'

Barnes swore under his breath. 'They share a vehicle. That's why he stole the pickup truck to move the bodies. She must've had the car to get to work.'

'Kay!' Carys raised her phone. 'The taxi company says Lenehan was a no-show. The driver arrived on time, but when he couldn't see Lenehan outside the hotel, he asked the night duty manager where he was. I phoned the hotel and got the number for the bloke. He remembered, because the taxi driver was fuming. Lenehan had been collected by one of those ride-sharing cars twenty minutes before.'

'What sort of car?'

'He's got no idea of the make or model – it was too dark to see, but he says it was a silver four-door—'

Kay spun around and swiped her card across the

locking mechanism to the interview room, Barnes at her heels.

The duty solicitor paused from talking to his client as Kay stormed across to the table, and Bettina's eyes widened.

'Bettina – you reported your car being stolen this morning. Why didn't you tell us?'

The woman's bottom lip quivered. 'I f-forgot. I was scared.'

'Tell me what happened.'

'I parked it outside our house as usual when I got back from the hotel the night before last. When I woke up yesterday morning, it had gone. Derek was out when I got home and didn't come back until last night, so I didn't see him. He was asleep when I woke up this morning and the car was still missing. He obviously hadn't used it, so I phoned the police to report it.' Tears streamed down the woman's cheeks. 'He was bloody livid when he woke up and I told him what I'd done. I've never seen him like that before.'

Dread wormed its way through Kay's body.

'Bettina, where is your husband right now?'

FIFTY-THREE

Half an hour later, Kay slammed shut the door to the pool car and hurried over to where Dave Morrison and Aaron Stewart stood next to their vehicle.

Their Kent Police-emblazoned car had beaten them there by mere minutes, its occupants out on patrol in the area when the call had been issued to arrest Derek Flinders.

'Any sign of him?'

'No.'

Kay pursed her lips as Barnes joined her. 'Had time to search the place?'

'Not yet. The workshop's locked. Should we tape it off?'

'In a moment. We'll take a look first. Give us a hand?'

He nodded and hurried over to where his colleague was radioing in an update to the command centre, and relayed Kay's instructions.

'Any news on whether Flinders has been arrested?'

'Nothing yet,' said Carys, and handed Kay a set of protective booties. 'I've asked Debbie to call my mobile in case we don't hear it over the radio.'

'Thanks.' She took a pair of disposable gloves Barnes held out to her and slipped them on. 'Okay. Let's take a look.'

She called over her shoulder. 'Dave – can you and Aaron head around the back in case he's here and tries to make a run for it? We're looking for a car, too.'

She gave them the make and model details and watched as the beams from their torches swept over the ground before them.

When they disappeared around the corner of the building, Kay led the way to the double doors at the front, ensuring the others followed in her footsteps and kept to a demarcated path. Harriet wouldn't thank her if they traipsed all over a potential crime scene.

Moonlight aided their approach, the summer night sky clear from clouds, a whisper of a breeze in the trees above their heads.

Kay tried to recall the liveliness of the surrounding area during the market and wondered what hellish events had taken place without the knowledge of those who frequented the centre.

For she was sure this was where the three men had died.

A shiver crawled down her spine, and she shook herself to lose the thoughts. She had to concentrate. They needed evidence, and they needed to ensure no-one else had been taken by Flinders. Bettina had assured them Patrick Lenehan was the last man she'd met with, but Kay wasn't leaving anything to chance.

'It's locked,' said Barnes, and pointed to a sturdy padlock that had been affixed to the metal latch. 'Hold this.'

Gavin took his torch while Barnes reached into his jacket pocket for his lock picks and set to work.

In moments, he'd released the lock and pulled open the right-hand door.

It moved with ease.

'He's kept the hinges well oiled,' said Carys.

'All right. You two keep back,' said Barnes, taking his torch from Gavin. 'Piper – come with me. We'll call when it's clear.'

Kay knew better than to argue. Instead, she and

Carys stood on the threshold and shone their torches into the gloom.

As Barnes and Gavin moved between the work-benches and shelves, Kay tried to batten down the adrenalin that was coursing through her body.

She had to remain calm for the sake of her team.

Beside her, Carys fidgeted from foot to foot, unable to temper her impatience, and Kay reached out a hand to still her. Neither said anything; they were too engrossed in watching their colleagues' progress through the workshop.

Suddenly, Barnes's voice carried across the void.

'Can one of you find a light switch? I can't see a bloody thing.'

They both sprang into action, and moments later a burst of light filled the space, and Kay blinked several times to clear her line of vision.

Barnes was on the far side of the room and switched off his torch as their eyes met.

'Nothing yet,' he said.

'Keep looking.'

'Guv.'

She spun round as Aaron Stewart appeared, and he beckoned to her.

'Found the car.'

'Carys, with me. Lead the way, Aaron.'

They followed him around the side of the shed to where Morrison stood, his gloved hand clutching the edge of a thick tarpaulin.

'Show me,' said Kay.

He lifted the tarpaulin away from the hulk it covered, exposing a car licence plate.

'Good. He hasn't had time to dispose of it. Get this off and open the back.'

She stood back while Morrison released the handle and the faint *whoosh* of hydraulics reached her ears as the back door to the vehicle lifted into the air.

Morrison aimed the beam from his torch into the dark interior and let out a triumphant bark.

'Look.' He leaned in and plucked a torn piece of fabric from a metal tyre lever, holding it up to the light in his gloved hand. A bloodstain covered one edge of the material. 'Someone was in here.'

'All right,' said Kay. 'Seal it off.'

The radio on Carys's vest chirped to life, and she turned up the volume. 'It's Hughes.'

'What is it?'

'We've got him, guv,' said the sergeant. 'Uniform arrested him at Charing Heath. Apparently, he was trying to flag down a car for a lift, but when he realised it was police, he took off. He had to be restrained – put up a hell of a fight.'

'Good work.'

'Kay!'

They all turned at the sound of Barnes's voice, and ran back to the workshop.

'What's wrong?' said Kay as she burst through the door.

Barnes stood in the middle of the space, and beckoned them over. 'Help me move the bench. There's something under here.'

'Piper, Carys – help him.'

The two detectives crossed the room to where Barnes stood and helped him drag the workbench across the floor.

'What's going on, Ian?'

In response, he pointed to the floor.

'I've seen something like this before, when I was a young copper,' he said. 'The suspect buried his victim on some abandoned ground. We only found it because the earth had settled after it rained. It dipped like this.'

Kay signalled to the two uniformed officers who stood hovering at the threshold. 'Step away. Get Harriet's team here as soon as possible. This floor is coming up. Now.'

They left the building at a run, the older of the

two holding his radio to his mouth as he relayed the instructions.

'Do we wait for Harriet?' said Carys.

Kay pondered the question. If she waited, she couldn't live with herself if another victim lay beneath the structure, waiting for someone to help.

'No,' she said eventually. 'Let's get these floor-boards removed.'

Gavin handed her a claw hammer. 'Found these over on the workbench over there. It'll make our job easier.'

'These nails are new, Kay,' said Barnes.

'He's replacing them each time,' she said as she applied the claw to the nearest of the nails. 'Whatever was down here wasn't meant to get out.'

They fell silent at her words, then crouched and worked at the nails hammered into the boards.

One by one, the planks were removed, and a faint noise reached them.

'What's that?' whispered Carys, then cried out.

A swarm of flies burst from the cavity, filling the workshop, and Kay swatted at them as they came too close to her face.

She peered at her colleagues. Each one of them looked shocked and disgusted as the insects buzzed around them before fleeing through the open doors.

'Kay, look.'

Her gaze dropped to the floorboard Gavin cradled in his lap, and Barnes swore under his breath.

A series of scratch marks were carved into the wood, dried blood streaking across the surface that had faced the ground.

'Someone was trying to escape,' she said.

The stench hit her next, and she took an involuntary step back from the hole that was starting to emerge in the floor.

'You said it once before,' said Carys, her eyes wide. 'It's fear.'

'It's death. This is where he was hiding the bodies,' said Barnes, his voice gruff.

'Ian – stay here,' said Kay. 'Carys, Gavin, get yourselves over to the door – no matter what happens, you stay there. We're not going to contaminate this scene more than we have to.'

She waited until her two colleagues were out of the way, then turned back to Barnes.

Without a word, Barnes nodded, then worked at the last of the floorboards, piling them behind where they crouched.

As they worked, Kay realised that the original concrete foundation had been chipped apart and a deep hole had been carved into the ground under the workshop floor.

She reckoned the crevice measured a little longer than the length of her own body and shivered.

Derek Flinders had made a coffin out of the floor of his workshop.

As the last floorboard came up in his hands, Barnes shoved it to one side and raised his gaze to Kay. 'Are you ready for this?'

'As I'll ever be.'

She took a deep breath before peering into the shallow hole they'd uncovered.

Whatever happened next, she knew she'd never forget.

She flipped her torch on, then swung it into the space below.

She recoiled from the bloody mess that lined the makeshift cavity, covering her face as a second swarm of flies lifted into the air, then blinked to try to lose the sight of the wriggling maggots that infested the space where Flinders had kept his victims' bodies before burning their remains.

'Bloody hell, I was right,' said Barnes.

FIFTY-FOUR

A chill crept across Kay's shoulders as she assessed their suspect.

The man sitting before her in the early hours of the morning gazed at her with deep green eyes from under a dark brown fringe. His expression was blank, giving nothing away, and giving no hint of the evil that had driven him to kill, dismember and burn three innocent men.

And those were the ones they knew about.

Under further questioning, Bettina Merriweather had provided names for two more men she'd slept with in the past year; men whose details appeared on the missing persons database, lost without a trace.

Derek Flinders had refused to provide details of a solicitor to represent him, and so a reluctant duty solicitor had attended, biting back a shocked retort after flipping through the notes Kay had passed to him in the corridor outside.

'State your name and address for the record,' said Barnes.

'Derek Flinders, Rosewell Cottage, Sutton Valence.'

'Are you the husband of Bettina Merriweather?'

'Yes.'

'Do you own or lease any other property, Mr Flinders?'

'I lease a workshop at the craft centre.'

'Does anyone else have access to that workshop?'

'No. I have the only key.'

Kay shoved a photograph across the desk depicting the crime scene that had been set up at the man's workshop overnight.

'Can you confirm this is the workshop you lease?'

'Yes.'

'Explain why we found traces of blood and faeces concealed beneath the floor.'

Flinders blinked. 'I have no idea what you're talking about.'

'How did you feel about your wife sleeping with the hotel guests?' said Kay.

A twitch began at the corner of Flinders' right eye,

and Kay edged backwards in her chair a split second before he launched from his seat and spat at the space where she'd been.

Barnes was on his feet before the door opened and Sergeant Hughes burst into the room.

Kay pushed back her chair as the two men restrained Flinders, the duty solicitor's face one of shock.

Kay's satisfaction at their suspect's response dwindled as he was returned to the desk, and she nodded her thanks to Hughes as he wiped down the surface with disinfectant before standing beside the desk in case Flinders tried anything else.

Now she'd gained an insight into the temper that lay beneath his calm demeanour, they had to glean enough information from him to support the evidence and press charges.

Barnes retook his place beside her and folded his arms on the table. 'Let's try again,' he said after requesting that Hughes cite his name, rank and number for the recording. 'Did you kill Patrick Lenehan?'

Flinders rolled his neck before his eyes locked on Barnes. 'Yes.'

'Why did you kill him?'

'Because he deserved it. He slept with my wife.'

'Did he tell you that?'

'Eventually.'

Kay noticed the panicked expression in the solicitor's eyes and felt sorry for the man.

Not only had he been dragged out of bed in the early hours of the morning to attend the police station, he now found himself representing a killer who seemed defiant in the face of accusation.

Remorseless, in fact.

In the silence that followed, the clock on the wall ticked the seconds away and Kay realised she would never be able to hear the noise again without recalling Flinders' chilling admission.

'Clive Wallis and Rupert Blacklock. Who were they to you?' said Barnes.

'They slept with my wife.'

'How do you know?'

Flinders sighed, shuffled in his chair and smiled benevolently.

'Because unknown to my wife, I realised what she was doing a long time ago. From time to time, she would lie and tell me she was working late. At first, I thought she was telling me the truth, that she was working an extra shift because we needed the money, but then I became suspicious when she came home late one night. I could smell him on her. Their sex. The next time she lied, I cycled over to the hotel, and I waited. Around the time her supposed shift would end, she left the hotel. I nearly missed her – she used a side door. Now, if she did have a late shift, why would she do that?' He didn't wait for an answer. 'After a while, a man appeared at the doors to the reception area. He was obviously expecting a taxi. I wheeled my bike over to him, and pretended I was arriving for work. I could smell her perfume on him. You can hear it in her voice these days, too – she gets excited when she tells me she has to work late. What sort of person gets excited about that?'

Flinders leaned forward and slammed his fist onto the table, and they jumped backwards. 'A liar. That's who. A liar.'

'Why the charcoal? Why burn those men's bodies once you'd dismembered them? Why not simply bury them?' said Kay.

An evil smile peeled back his lips. 'Because she always insists on having barbecues in the summer. What a perfect way to use them. What a perfect way to serve them up.'

Kay swallowed, fighting down bile, and she knew from the grunt Barnes emitted that he too was struggling with what they were hearing.

Finally, when she was able, she raised her eyes to Flinders once more.

'Do you mean to say you served her the remains of the men you murdered?'

'No comment.'

Kay gritted her teeth and pressed on. 'The construction works at the hotel – that's why you had to move the bodies in the pickup truck, wasn't it?'

He snorted in response. 'They weren't meant to pull down the old outbuildings until the end of the year. They said the expansion was on hold, so I was perfectly safe there. No-one would have known. I had all the time in the world. And then Bettina overheard someone talking in the reception area of the hotel and realised the demolition works weren't on hold after all – only the construction was.'

'Why did you steal the pickup truck?'

He sighed, as if it were an inconvenience to have to explain. 'Because my wife uses the car for work. I can only use it when she gets home. I cycle to the craft centre. I could hardly move a body that way, could I? Anyway,' he said, contemplating a fingernail. 'I knew Alan wouldn't report it as missing. He's been bragging for the past two years he hasn't paid road tax for it, so he was hardly going to phone you up, was he? More's the pity the suspension was broken though. I wouldn't have lost the damn foot otherwise.'

'Why did you use your wife's car to transport Lenehan?' said Barnes.

Flinders' eyes gleamed. 'I thought she might appreciate the irony. Besides, it was easy. She was so tired from having sex with him that she was asleep within minutes of getting home. I simply took the car and drove back to the hotel where he was waiting for a taxi – there are so many ride-sharing cars around the area, he thought nothing of it when I turned up.'

'Tell me about Bristol.'

'What about it?'

'Bettina has confirmed she was sleeping with hotel guests while she worked there. What did you do with the bodies?'

A sly smile stretched across his face. 'No comment.'

Kay leaned back in her chair and contemplated the man before her. 'We have enough evidence to charge you for the murders of three men, and we will lay further charges once our enquiries are complete, Mr Flinders. Don't you have any remorse for what you've done?'

'I told you. They deserved it – they slept with my wife.'

'You spared her,' said Kay.

'She's mine. She belongs to me. No-one else.'

'And yet she slept with all of them.'

Flinders clenched his fists but remained silent.

A few minutes later, the initial interview was over and Kay and Barnes stood outside in the corridor, shell-shocked.

'We'll conclude the interview once I've had a chance to discuss the charges with Jude Martin at the Crown Prosecution Service,' said Kay, 'but I've never met anyone so evil in my life. I mean, he enjoyed what he did to those men. And as for what he might have been doing with the remains—'

Barnes ran his hand over weary eyes and sighed. 'Any normal person would get a divorce.'

FIFTY-FIVE

'Do you think she knew?' said Carys as they watched Hughes lead Bettina away to the cells.

'Yes. I do,' said Kay. 'I think she chose to ignore what was happening though. I think she probably thought it was convenient that those men disappeared without a trace.'

They walked towards the stairwell, and back up to the incident room. Sunlight streamed through the windows, and Kay suppressed a yawn.

'I wonder why she didn't confront him about it?' said Carys.

'Maybe she was scared of having her suspicions confirmed,' said Kay.

'Or, she was scared he'd kill her,' said Gavin.

Kay pushed through the door, and made her way

over to the whiteboard, her gaze flickering over the victims' photographs while the buzz of activity around her continued.

Sharp had written Patrick Lenehan's name in the space beneath the large question mark she'd drawn after the discovery of the third body, and she realised that he had probably taken it upon himself to get photographs of the rings and belt buckle identified by the Irishman's family with the help of the Cork-based Garda.

On cue, the DCI peered out of his office. 'Good, you're here. Where's Barnes?'

'Getting a coffee from the canteen. He'll be here in a minute.'

'Let's get the final briefing underway as soon as he gets here. I think everyone deserves an early finish, given it's the weekend.'

They waited near the whiteboard while their colleagues grabbed cans of energy drink from the canteen vending machine or coffee – anything to keep them going for the final throes of the investigation – and then Sharp gave a short whistle to gain their attention and gestured to Kay to begin.

'I want to thank you all for your time and dedication given to this case,' she said, making sure she made eye contact with each and every one of her colleagues. 'I know some of you have young children at home and it hasn't been easy with the hours we've been keeping, but it's your efforts that have got us this result. You should be proud of yourselves.'

A smattering of applause filled the room.

'Derek Flinders has been charged with the murders of Clive Wallis, Rupert Blacklock, and Patrick Lenehan. From Monday, we'll begin to work with the Crown Prosecution Service to ensure he receives the longest sentence possible when the case comes before the courts. We'll also be working with our colleagues at Avon and Somerset to find out if he was responsible for the cold cases they have. Be prepared for a busy week, but in the meantime go home and enjoy the rest of the weekend with your families. Guv, do you have anything you want to add?'

Sharp looked up from his notes. 'First of all, to add to what Kay's already said, this has to be one of the most harrowing investigations some of you have experienced in your careers to date.'

He nodded at Debbie before he continued.

'You all make a difference to this team, and I know you all talk between yourselves. But – and this is important – if the circumstances of these murders are troubling you, then seek help. It can be done anonymously, but for goodness' sake don't try to cope on your own, all right?'

'Guv.'

'Yes, guv.'

Sharp put down his notes on the table behind him, then turned to face the room once more. 'Now we've got that out of the way, I have an announcement to make. As you're all aware, Kay and I have spent the last few weeks interviewing potential candidates for the role of Detective Sergeant. It hasn't been easy, as we're such a tight-knit group and it's imperative we found someone who could fill the role with minimum disruption. I'm happy to announce we've found the perfect person for the job.'

Confused, Kay swung around to face him. 'We have?'

He winked. 'We have. Ian Barnes, congratulations on your promotion.'

Kay's shocked gasp was drowned out by her colleagues' cheers and whistles as they crowded around Barnes.

From his position next to the window, he caught her eye and grinned before wandering over to where she stood.

'You sly bastard,' she said, shaking his hand. 'Why didn't you tell me you'd changed your mind?'

He laughed. 'I wanted it to be a surprise. Besides, you've had enough to think about lately with this case.'

'I'm glad you took the job.'

'Me too. It would've been weird having a complete stranger join the team, wouldn't it?'

The team milled around them, calling out good-byes and heading for the exit, and she glanced over Barnes's shoulder to where Gavin and Carys were packing up their desks.

He turned to see what she was looking at. 'Do you think they'll be okay? I mean, it wasn't their fault Derek Flinders hoodwinked us all, but I'm not sure they realise that.'

Kay watched Gavin patting Carys on the back as he opened the door for her and they disappeared from view. 'Yes, they'll be okay. They're a good team, those two.'

'Right, well I'll be off, too. See you Monday?'

'Bright eyed and bushy tailed.'

Half an hour later, Kay steered her car into the late Saturday morning traffic and pointed it in the direction of home.

She lowered the window and let the breeze whip at her hair, clearing the fog from her mind as she drove along the A20 towards Bearsted.

She stifled a yawn. The adrenalin that had kept her going the past few days was rapidly wearing off.

As she swung the car into the lane that bisected the modern housing estate from the older part of Weavering, she braked to negotiate the final corner and then sighed as she pulled into the driveway of her house.

'Thank God. Home,' she mumbled, barely managing to climb from the car.

A spasm seized her aching back muscles. She'd treat herself to a long soak in the bath later. Somehow, she didn't think she'd be able to keep her eyes open long enough to read a book afterwards.

She turned her key in the lock to the front door and dumped her bag on the stairs.

'I'm home!'

Adam poked his head around the kitchen door, his face a picture of misery.

'Before you say anything, I'm sorry, all right?'

Kay's heart sank, wondering what on earth had happened. All she wanted to do was kick off her heels, put on a pair of shorts and sit out on the patio with a very large glass of cold white wine.

'What's going on? What's wrong?' She hurried into the kitchen as he moved back to the worktop and held up a tattered collection of rags. 'Hang on. Isn't that the dress I was going to wear to Abby's birthday party?'

Adam nodded, his cheeks flushing as red as the fabric.

'Misha got out. She ate the washing that was hanging on the line.'

THE END

Dear Reader,

First of all, I wanted to say a huge thank you for choosing to read *Gone to Ground*. I hope you enjoyed the story.

The idea for the book evolved from a visit I made to Kent a few years ago to visit family. We went for a walk along the Pilgrim's Way between Harrietsham and Hollingbourne, and when approaching a copse of trees to the left of the path, I spotted smoke.

Drawing near, I saw the ghostly shape of a man partially hidden beside a corrugated iron structure and when I got back to the house and investigated online, I discovered he was probably making charcoal.

The image of this ghostly figure amongst the

smoke stayed with me, and so became the method of disposal used by the serial killer in this story.

If you did enjoy *Gone to Ground*, I'd be grateful if you could write a review. It doesn't have to be long, just a few words, but it is the best way for me to help new readers discover one of my books for the first time.

If you'd like to stay up to date with my new releases, as well as exclusive competitions and give-aways, you're welcome to join my Reader Group at my website, www.rachelamphlett.com.

You can also contact me via Facebook, Twitter, or by email. I love hearing from readers – I read every message and will always reply.

Thanks again for your support.

Best wishes,

Rachel Amphlett

CPSIA information can be obtained
at www.ICGtesting.com
Printed in the USA
BVHW03s0039020718
520586BV00001B/16/P